Book of the Film

Copyright ' 2006 Disney Enterprises, Inc./Pixar.Disney/Pixar elements
' Disney/Pixar; Hudson Hornet is a trademark of DaimlerChrysler;
Volkswagen trademarks, design patents and copyrights are used with the
approval of the owner, Volkswagen AG; Model T is a registered trademark
of Ford Motor Company; Fiat is a trademark of Fiat S.p.A.; Mack is a
registered trademark of Mack Trucks, Inc.; Chevrolet Impala is a trademark
of General Motors; Porsche is a trademark of Porsche; Jeep is a registered
trademark of DaimlerChrysler; Plymouth Superbird is a trademark of
DaimlerChrysler; Ferrari elements are trademarks of Ferrari S.p.A.; Petty
marks used by permission of Petty Marketing LLC.

This is a Parragon book
First published in 2006

Parragon
Queen Street House
4 Queen Street
Bath, BA1 1HE, UK
ISBN 1-40547-216-2
Printed in China

Copyright ' 2006 Disney Enterprises, Inc.\Pixar Animation Studios

All rights reserved.
No part of this publication may be reproduced, stored in a retrieval system, or
transmitted by any means, mechanical, photocopying, recording, or otherwise,
without prior permission of the copyright holder.

Book of the Film

Adapted by Lisa Papademetriou

Excitement pulsed through a packed stadium where thousands of revved-up fans gathered to watch the Dinoco 400 – the biggest race of the year. They honked their horns and waved their flags in support of their favourite racers. The winner would receive the Piston Cup trophy and be crowned champion for the entire season!

While more fans cheered outside, Lightning McQueen, the rookie, was parked in the back of his posh trailer, trying to prepare himself for the race. It had been a huge year for McQueen. He had exploded onto the racing scene like a stick of dynamite, and he already had an impressive list of wins and top finishes. He knew that he had a good shot at winning the Dinoco 400 and, if he did, he would be the first rookie in history to do it. McQueen felt his rpm increase at the thought.

"Focus." He concentrated hard. "Speed. I am speed. I eat losers for breakfast. I am Lightning." He had two things on his mind: winning and all the perks that came with it, including the Dinoco sponsorship. The sponsorship meant that Dinoco would pay McQueen a lot of money to compete in races.

"Hey, Lightning," called Mack. He was McQueen's loyal trailer driver. "You ready?"

McQueen could feel the roar of the crowds in the stands as his tyres buzzed.

"Oh, yeah!" The sleek red racing car revved his engine. "Lightning's ready."

Cameras flashed across the stands like fireworks as McQueen rolled off the back of his trailer. He made sure he gave them a good look at his lucky lightning-bolt sticker and the number 95 on his side.

"*Ka-chow!*" he called out as his grille flashed across the stadium's giant video screen.

McQueen made his way to the track. His competitors were waiting. There were more than 40 other cars in the race, but Lightning McQueen knew that he had to worry about only two of them. Strip Weathers – also known as The King – had won more Piston Cups than any other car in history. He had also been Dinoco's golden boy for years, getting all those big pay cheques. This would be his last race before retiring. McQueen was sure that The King wanted to go out on top, and he still had the speed to do it.

And then there was Chick Hicks. He was famous for battling through the line – bashing any car who stood in his way. He had never managed to beat The King, though. He was more determined than ever to win and begin a new era – the Chick era.

"Bob, my oil pressure's through the roof right now!" cried Darrell Cartrip, one of the race announcers. Poor Darrell was in danger of overheating as the green flag dropped. The three rivals lurched into high gear, launching the greatest race of the decade as they roared across the starting line.

"Right you are, Darrell," Bob Cutlass agreed as

he watched the action from the announcers' booth. "The winner of this race will win the season title *and* the Piston Cup!"

"The legend, the runner-up and the rookie," Darrell said. "Three cars, one champion."

Lightning McQueen pushed up the speed as The King's sleek tail fin flashed around the track with Chick right behind it. McQueen punched the gas and flew ahead of Chick. But Chick Hicks wasn't about to lose this race to a rookie. Coming up fast, he slammed McQueen's rear and spun him onto the infield.

The crowd gasped as McQueen whirled out of control on the grass.

McQueen recovered quickly, tearing up the field as he zipped back onto the track. But now he was in last place! He pushed hard to make up the time.

Still, Chick wasn't going to let McQueen close in on him. He wasn't taking any chances. "Dinoco is all mine!" he cried as he slammed into the car beside him, sending it spinning out of control. In an instant, other cars began to crash, causing a pile-up. "Get through *that,* McQueen!" With a confident sneer, the ruthless race car headed into the pits for fuel and service.

McQueen tried to go around the pile-up, but it was impossible. With no other choice, he did the only thing he could think of: he went through it! Dodging rubble and smoke, McQueen moved spectacularly, gliding between stopped vehicles and leapfrogging into the air over a pile of cars.

"McQueen made it through!" shouted Chick's crew chief.

And McQueen didn't stop. While everyone else headed into the pits, he kept rolling . . . right into first place!

"Woo-hoo!" McQueen cried.

"You know, the rookie just fired his crew chief," Darrell announced. "That's the third one this season!"

"Well, he says he likes working alone, Darrell!" Bob said.

Chick and The King bolted out of pit row and didn't waste any time in trying to catch up with McQueen. The laps flew by and it looked as if no one would beat him. Finally, McQueen headed into the pits for fuel. He couldn't win the race on fumes. "No, no, no – no tyres!" he shouted as his crew tried to replace his worn tyres. There wasn't any time. "Just the gas!"

"Looks like it's all gas 'n' goes for McQueen today!" Darrell observed as he peered down at pit row below him. "Now, normally I'd say that's a short-term gain, long-term loss, but it sure is working for him."

The frenzied crowd's excitement grew as the contenders sped around the track. Then the white flag waved.

LAST LAP, read the stadium's giant video monitor.

"Checkered flag," McQueen said to himself, "here I come."

Ka-blam!

"Oh, no," Darrell cried as he watched the rookie lose speed. "McQueen has blown a tyre!"

Chick and The King pounded ahead, making up time with every second. But McQueen didn't give up. He plunged forwards . . . .

Ka-blam!

He lost another tyre!

"Come on!" Determined to win, McQueen struggled on, limping on his rear-wheel rims.

"I don't believe what I'm watching!" Darrell cried. "Lightning McQueen is 100 feet from his Piston Cup–"

"The King and Chick are coming on strong!" Bob shouted. "McQueen's nearly there, but Chick and The King are almost caught up!"

McQueen dragged himself forward. He was inches away from crossing the finish line – and making history. He could hear Chick and The King coming up behind him. In a last-ditch effort, McQueen took a giant leap and slid forward. He even stuck out his tongue to gain an extra inch.

"It's too close to call!" Bob announced as he gaped at the photo finish. "The most spectacular, amazing, incomprehensible, unequivocally unbelievable ending in the history of the world, and we don't even know who won!"

McQueen let his pit crew fit him with a new set of tyres while the referees reviewed the instant replay. The rookie wasn't worried; he was positive he had the race in the bag.

"We're here in Victory Lane awaiting the race results," announced a reporter as she thrust a microphone into McQueen's grille. "McQueen, that was quite a risky move, not taking tyres. Are you sorry you don't have a crew chief?"

McQueen gave her a cocky smile. "No, I'm not," he replied. "'Cause I'm a one-man show."

The reporter turned to the camera. "That was a very confident Lightning McQueen, coming to you live from Victory Lane."

"Yo, Chuck," McQueen called to one of his pit

crew, who was struggling to replace the blown tyres. "Chuck! What are you doing? You're blocking the camera. Everyone wants to see the bolt," he said, referring to his lucky lightning-bolt sticker. Suddenly, the jack flew out from underneath McQueen. *Ka-thunk!* He hit the ground hard.

"Whoa," he called as the pittie started to leave, "where are you going?"

"I quit, Mr One-Man Show!" the pittie spat.

"Oh, oh, okay, leave!" McQueen grinned at the camera. "Fine!" He snorted and added sarcastically, "How will I ever find anyone else who knows how to fill me up with gas? Adios, Chuck!"

"And my name's not Chuck!" the pittie hollered.

"Whatever," McQueen scoffed. Plenty of pit crews had quit on him before, but Lightning McQueen didn't care. He knew that when it came to racing, he was the only one who mattered.

"Hey, Lightning," Chick called as he rolled up to his rival. "Yo, McQueen. Seriously, that was some pretty darn nice racing out there . . . by *me*."

"Good one!" his pit crew said, cracking up at the lame joke. "Oh, yeah! Zinger!"

"Welcome to the Chick era, baby," Chick went on, his voice glossy with confidence. "The Piston Cup, it's mine, dude, it's mine. Hey, fellas, how do you think I'd look in Dinoco blue?"

"Blue's your colour," one of the pitties piped up.

"In your dreams," McQueen replied, "thunder."

"Yeah, right, *thunder*," Chick said, turning to his pit crew. "What's he talking about, thunder'?"

"Hey, you know," McQueen shot back, "because thunder always comes after lightning! *Ka-pow!*" McQueen flashed his shiny lightning-bolt sticker at the crowd again, and the reporters went wild. They squeezed in around him, angling for a photo of the famous racing car. "McQueen, over here!" "This way, McQueen!" "Hey, McQueen, we want to see the bolt!"

"*Ka-ching!*" McQueen said with each new pose for the cameras. "*Ch-ch-chkow!*"

Chick turned to his pit crew as the reporters elbowed him and his crew out of the way. "Who here knew about the *thunder* thing?" he demanded.

The King stood nearby, surrounded by his loyal Dinoco pit crew.

"You sure made Dinoco proud, King," said Dinoco's owner, Tex, to his long-time companion.

"My pleasure, Tex," The King replied.

The King's wife snuggled against his fender. "Whatever happens," she said gently, "you're a winner to me, you ol' daddy rabbit."

"Thanks, dear," the veteran said lovingly. "Wouldn't be nothin' without you." Then he rolled over to McQueen, who was surrounded by adoring fans. The King knew that McQueen was arrogant, but he respected McQueen's talent. He wanted to help the kid.

"Hey, buddy," The King said, when the reporters had cleared away, "you're one gutsy racer. You got more talent in one lug nut than a lotta cars got in their whole body...."

"Really?" McQueen flushed with pride. *The King sure knows quality racing when he sees it*, the rookie thought. "Oh, that, that's–"

"But you're stupid," The King finished.

McQueen blinked. "Excuse me?"

"This ain't a one-man deal, kid," The King said. "You need to wise up and get yourself a good crew chief and a good team. You ain't gonna win unless you got good folks behind you and you let them do their job like they should. It's like I tell the boys at the shop: it's about everybody comin' together and doin' the best they can."

"Uh, yeah, that is spectacular advice," McQueen said absently. He wasn't really paying attention to what The King was saying. He was too busy picturing himself as the next Dinoco car, his face on the cover of magazines, his signature on the side of the company helicopter, fame, fortune and more Piston Cups than he could fit into his enormous mansion. And it was all starting right there, right then, with that win. "Thank you, Mr The King."

Just then, music sounded over the PA system. "Ladies and gentlemen," Bob announced, "for the first time in Piston Cup history . . ."

". . . a rookie has won the Piston Cup!" McQueen shouted. "Yes!" Revving his engine, he drove forward, bursting through the victory banner. He struck his finish-line pose for the crowd.

". . . we have a three-way tie!" Bob finished.

Confetti cannons burst, showering bits of paper

through the air like snowflakes. The King and Chick drove forward to join McQueen.

"Oh, boy!" Chick sniggered. "Hey, McQueen, that must be really embarrassing!"

McQueen scowled.

"Piston Cup officials have determined that a tiebreaker race between the three leaders will be held in California in one week," Bob announced.

McQueen was shocked. He couldn't believe that he hadn't won!

"Hey, rook," Chick whispered to McQueen, "first one to California gets Dinoco all to himself!"

McQueen slunk away, dejected. "'First one to California gets Dinoco all to himself'," he muttered. "Oh, we'll see who gets there first, Chick."

"**H**ey, kid!" Mack called as McQueen headed toward him. "Congrats on the tie!"

"I don't want to talk about it," the rookie replied grumpily. "C'mon, let's go, Mack. Saddle up. What'd you do with my trailer?"

"I parked it over at your sponsor's tent," Mack said. "You gotta make your personal appearance."

McQueen groaned. His sponsor was Rust-eze Medicated Bumper Ointment, and the tent was always filled with rusty old cars. McQueen would have preferred something flashier, like Dinoco, but it was Rust-eze that had given him his big break. And a contract was a contract. He had to make a personal appearance, and that was that. He forced a smile and drove into the tent.

"Nothing soothes a rusty bumper like Rust-eze,"

McQueen's recorded image said over a plasma TV screen in the back of the tent. "Wow, look at that shine! Use Rust-eze and you, too, can look like me. *Ka-chow*!"

The racing car heaved a sigh as he watched his bosses – two brothers who were the owners of Rust-eze – tell their usual bad jokes. The rusty cars who filled the tent laughed their bumpers off at everything the two brothers said.

"I remember this car from Swampscott," one brother said to the crowd, "he was so rusty, he didn't even cast a shadow!"

The assembled cars hooted and honked as soon as they saw their hero.

"*Ecck* . . . I hate rusty cars," McQueen muttered under his breath. "This is *not* good for my image." He slunk behind a cardboard cut-out of himself, trying to hide.

"Hey, look, there he is!" one of the brothers cried, catching sight of McQueen.

"Our almost-champ!" the other shouted. "Get your rear end in here, kid!"

A spotlight flashed onto McQueen. He made his

way through the rusty cars, greeted the crowd and forced himself to laugh at his bosses' jokes. Finally, it was time for him to go.

"Aw, we love you," his boss said as McQueen backed into his trailer, "and we're lookin' forward to another great year – just like this year!"

McQueen smiled. Then the gate crashed down. "Not on your life," he grumbled.

Mack hitched himself to the trailer, and soon he was taking Lightning McQueen west. His face appeared on a video link inside Lightning's trailer.

"California, here we come!" Mack sang.

"Dinoco, here we come!" McQueen said to himself as he scanned the trophies and plaques that lined the walls and shelves of his trailer. He couldn't wait to land the glamorous new sponsor.

Just as McQueen had settled under the buffer for a massage, the phone rang.

"Is this the world's fastest racing machine?" asked a smooth voice at the other end of the line.

McQueen perked up at the sound of his agent's voice. "Is that you, Harv? Buddy!"

"Kid," Harv replied, "it is such an honour to be your agent that it almost hurts me to take ten per cent of your winnings . . . and merchandising. And ancillary rights in perpetuity. Anyway, what a race, huh, champ? Didn't see it, but I heard you were great. Listen, they're giving you 20 tickets for the tiebreaker thing in Cali. I'll pass 'em on to your friends; you shoot me the names."

"Right. Friends." McQueen paused. Who was there to invite? The truth was, he had tons of fans . . . but he couldn't think of any real friends. He was speechless.

"Okay, I get it, Mr Popular," Harv broke in. "So many friends you can't narrow it down."

McQueen didn't bother to correct him.

"Okay, gotta jump, kid," Harv said. "Let me know how it goes."

Harv hung up and McQueen's eyes wandered to the window. A van with a mattress tied to its roof struggled to pass them.

Many long hours later, McQueen was becoming more and more impatient. *Can t we go any faster?* he wondered. "Oh, come on, Mack," he complained over the intercom. "You're in the slow lane. This is Lightning McQueen you're hauling here."

Mack headed toward a lorry stop. "Just stopping off for a quick breather, kid," he explained. "Ol' Mack needs a rest."

"Absolutely not!" McQueen insisted. "We're driving straight through all night until we get to California. We agreed to it."

Mack groaned. "All night? May I remind you, federal DOT regs state–"

"C'mon, Mack." McQueen's voice softened. "I need to get there before Chick and hang with Dinoco." McQueen really wanted to keep going.

Mack looked at the lorry stop, where a line of lorries slept peacefully. "Hey, kid," Mack said gently, "I don't know if I can make it."

"Oh, sure you can, Mack!" McQueen said brightly. "Look, it'll be easy. I'll stay up with you! All night long."

Finally, Mack agreed to keep going down the dark Interstate road.

McQueen kept Mack company for a short while, until he fell asleep. Mack travelled the endless miles alone. The lines dividing the lanes rolled like ribbons under his tyres, and soon he felt his headlights drooping.

Mack was desperately trying to shake himself awake when a group of flashy cars rolled up beside him. Boost, the leader, noticed that Mack was falling asleep and decided to have some fun. "We got ourselves a nodder," he told the other cars.

DJ, a car with enormous speakers, put on some soothing music.

"Pretty music," Mack said sleepily. He let out a huge yawn. Soon he was snoring as he rolled along.

"Yo, Wingo!" Boost called as he bumped Mack towards his friend. "Lane change, man!"

"Right back at ya!" Wingo said as he booted Mack back across the road. But Boost swerved out of the way, allowing Mack to bump onto the hard shoulder.

"Oops, I missed," Boost said, and the other cars sniggered.

Inside McQueen's trailer, the jostling caused a trophy to slip off the shelf. It hit the lift control button and the back door fell open. McQueen rolled to the lip of the ramp as Mack, still fast asleep, veered back onto the road.

Suddenly, Snot Rod felt a sneeze coming on. "*Ahh . . . Ahh . . . Ahh . . . Ahh–*"

"He's gonna blow!" Wingo cried.

Ah-chooo! Snot Rod sneezed, sending a burst of flame from his exhaust pipe.

Mack swerved as he was startled awake. "Gesundheit!" he said automatically – then he realized where he was. "Whoa! One should never drive while drowsy." He didn't know that in the commotion McQueen had been shaken off the ramp! Mack kept driving into the night, leaving McQueen alone on the road.

Honk!

"Get out of the way!" cried a car as he sped around the sleeping McQueen – who had just rolled into oncoming traffic. "You're going the wrong way! Ahhhh!"

Cars honked and shouted as they swerved to avoid McQueen.

"Mack!" McQueen hollered, swerving just in time to avoid an oncoming lorry.

Turning sharply, McQueen dodged through the traffic after his trailer, who still hadn't noticed that the racing car was missing. But McQueen couldn't see where he was going. Racing cars drove only on racetracks – and the racetracks were always lit up – so McQueen didn't have real headlights. "Mack!" he cried, momentarily losing sight of the trailer. "Mack, wait for me!"

But Mack was too far ahead; he couldn't hear McQueen.

McQueen was gaining ground. He followed the trailer's rear lights as it headed to a slip road. Leaving the Interstate for a country road, the trailer rumbled over some train tracks. McQueen sped up –

and jumped the crossing a millisecond before a train came through!

But when McQueen pulled up beside the trailer, he made a horrible discovery. The trailer he'd been following wasn't Mack at all.

"Turn on your lights, you moron," the trailer yelled at McQueen.

"Mack . . ." McQueen whispered to himself as the trailer drove away. So . . . if that trailer wasn't Mack, where could Mack be? "The Interstate," McQueen said. He turned and spotted some lights. He tore towards them at top speed, not realizing that he was heading for winding old Highway 66, not the Interstate.

A siren blasted through the night air and McQueen saw red and blue flashing lights. A police car! "Maybe he can help me," McQueen said, slowing down.

But the police car was old, and he hadn't had to chase a sleek young racing car for years. *Ka-blam*! He backfired.

"He's shooting at me!" McQueen said, panicking and putting his pedal to the metal. "Why's he shooting at me?"

Boom! *Boom*! *Ka-blam*! "I haven't gone this fast in years," the Sheriff said to himself as he sped after McQueen. "I'm gonna blow a gasket!"

Thinking he was being gunned down, McQueen swerved, snakelike, to avoid the blasts.

"What in the blue blazes?" cried the Sheriff. "Crazy hot-rodder."

McQueen and the Sheriff sped towards the sleepy little town of Radiator Springs. It was perfectly quiet there, and the locals were all gathered at Flo's V8 CafØ, looking up at the town's lone traffic light.

"I'm telling you, man," said Fillmore, an aging bus. "Every third blink is slower."

An old army jeep called Sarge gave Fillmore a dubious look. "The 60s weren't good to you, were they?"

Blam! *Blam*! *Ka-blam*!

Tyres squealed and the siren wailed as McQueen tore towards town with the Sheriff right on his bumper. As McQueen approached the traffic light, he got his first real look at Radiator Springs.

"What?" the racing car cried. "That's not the

Interstate! Ow!" He slammed into some traffic cones. "Ow! Ow! Ow!" McQueen swerved to avoid the cones and found himself heading straight for a barbed-wire fence! "No-no-no-no-no!" He burst through the fence with the wire wrapped around him. He dragged the fence forwards as he ploughed past the cafØ.

"I'm not the only one seeing this, right?" Fillmore asked as he stared at the out-of-control racing car in disbelief.

McQueen fishtailed, hitting some oil cans and a stack of tyres. Then he ground the garden of Red, the fire engine, into the dirt. He swerved to avoid the statue of the town's founder, Stanley, but the barbed wire caught it. For a moment, McQueen was pinned, spinning his wheels in place against the weight of the heavy statue, but then he revved the engine. The statue tipped over, landing in front of McQueen.

"*Ahhh!*" McQueen screamed, driving away, dragging Stanley and the barbed-wire fence behind him and ripping up the road. Veering to the side, the statue launched off a flat-bed trailer like a water-skier and landed in some telephone wires.

McQueen tried to get free, but he was still tangled in the barbed wire with Stanley. Suddenly, Stanley flew backwards, as if flung from a giant catapult.

"Fly away, Stanley," Fillmore called as the statue sailed overhead. "Be free."

The statue landed back on its pedestal and McQueen got tangled even more in a set of low-hanging telephone wires.

The winded sheriff drove up to McQueen, who was hanging upside down by the poles. "Boy," the Sheriff said, catching his breath. "You're in a heap of trouble."

With a sigh, McQueen's engine sputtered to a stop. He had passed out.

When McQueen opened his eyes the next morning, he could hardly make out the blurry shape in front of him.

"Oh, boy . . ." McQueen said groggily. "Where am I? What–?"

McQueen squinted. It took him a moment to work out what he was looking at: a rusty old breakdown lorry staring at him through a chain-link fence.

"Morning, Sleepin' Beauty!" the breakdown lorry sang. "Aha! Boy, I was wonderin' when you was gonna wake up!"

"*Ahh!*" McQueen cried, startled. "T-t-take whatever you want! Just don't hurt me!" He revved his engine, but he didn't move. He looked down at his tyre. "A parking boot?" he cried in horror at the wheel clamp that pinned him in place. "Why do I have a parking boot on? What do you . . . what's going on here, please?"

The breakdown lorry burst into a gap-toothed grin. "You're funny," he said. "I like you already! My name's Mater!"

McQueen was so surprised by the strange name that he stopped struggling against his wheel clamp. "Mater?"

"Yeah, like 'tuh-mater,'" the lorry explained, "but without the 'tuh.' What's your name?"

"What?" McQueen asked. "Look, I need to get to California as fast as possible. Where am I?"

"Where are ya?" Mater asked. "Shoot. You're in Radiator Springs, the cutest little town in Carburettor County."

McQueen looked around. All he could see was a dreary row of boarded-up buildings. It didn't look very cute to him. "Oh, great," he said sarcastically. "Just great!"

"Well, if you think that's great," Mater said proudly, "you should see the rest of the town!"

McQueen was starting to realize that Mater

wasn't the fastest car on the racetrack, which gave him an idea. "You know," McQueen said craftily, "I'd love to see the rest of the town, so if you could just open the gate, take this boot off, you and me – we go cruisin', check out the local scene, you know?"

"Dadgum!" Mater cried. "Cool!" He started to open the gate when a shout stopped him in his tracks.

"Mater!" bellowed the Sheriff as he rolled up. "What did I tell you about talking to the accused?"

Mater looked sheepish. "To not to."

"Well, quit your yappin'," the Sheriff snarled, "and tow this delinquent road hazard to traffic court."

"The Radiator Springs Traffic Court will come to order!" the Sheriff called as McQueen rolled into the front of the courtroom, his wheel clamp clanking.

The townsfolk were gathered in the courtroom – and they were not happy.

"Hey," called Ramone, a lowrider with a flashy paint job. "You scratched my paint. I ought to take a blowtorch to you, man!"

"Did you see what he did to my Stanley?" cried Lizzie, the oldest resident of the town.

A glamorous show car frowned at McQueen, indignant. "You see what he did to my cafØ?" Flo demanded. "Now I've gotta restack the cans."

"You broke the road," scolded the small Italian import named Luigi. He owned Luigi's Casa Della Tyres – and the tyres McQueen had ploughed through the night before. "You're a very bad car."

"Fascist!" Fillmore called.

"Commie!" bellowed Sarge.

"Officer, talk to me, babe," McQueen said to the Sheriff in a smooth voice. "How long is this gonna take? I gotta get to California, pronto."

"Where's your lawyer?" the Sheriff demanded.

"I don't know," McQueen admitted. "Tahiti, maybe?"

"When a defendant has no lawyer, the court will assign one to him. Hey!" the Sheriff called out to the assembled cars. "Anyone want to be his lawyer?"

"Shoot," Mater said. "I'll do it, Sheriff!"

McQueen groaned.

"All rise," Sheriff called. "The Honorable Doc Hudson presiding! May Doc have mercy on your soul."

An old blue car rolled into court and took his place at the judge's bench. "All right," Doc ranted, "I want to know who's responsible for wrecking my town, Sheriff. I want his hood on a platter. I'm going to put him in jail till he rots – no, check that. I'm gonna put him in jail till the jail rots on top of him and then I'm going to move him to a new jail and let that one rot. I'm–" Doc stopped short, narrowing his eyes as he got a good look at McQueen.

The racing car laughed nervously.

"Throw him out of here, Sheriff," Doc said in an official voice. "I want him out of my courtroom. I want him out of our town. Case dismissed!"

"Yes!" McQueen cried as the townsfolk gasped.

"Boy," Mater said to himself. "I'm pretty good at this lawyering stuff."

Just then, a sleek blue sports car drove into the courtroom. "Sorry I'm late, Your Honour," she said.

"Holy Porsche," McQueen muttered, awestruck by the gorgeous car. "She's gotta be from my attorney's office. Hey, thanks for coming," he said suavely, "but we're all set. He's letting me go."

"He's letting you go?" she repeated.

"Yeah, your job's pretty easy today," McQueen grinned. "All you have to do now is stand there and let me look at you. Listen, I'm going to cut to the chase. Me. You. Dinner." He flashed his lightning-bolt sticker. "*Ka-chow!*"

"Ow!" the blue sports car cried as the reflected

light shone in her pretty headlight eyes.

"I know," McQueen growled, moving closer to her. "I get that reaction a lot." He revved his engine.

"Okay . . ." she said, unimpressed. She excused herself to talk to the judge.

"Do what you gotta do, baby," McQueen told her. "Oh, but listen, be careful. Folks around here are not firing on all cylinders, if you know what I mean."

"I'll keep that in mind," the blue sports car replied as she rolled forward. "Hey there, Mater," she added as she drove past the breakdown lorry.

"Howdy, Sally," Mater replied.

McQueen gaped. "You know her?"

"She's the town attorney," Mater explained. "And my fiancØe."

"What?" McQueen cried.

"*Naah*, just kiddin'," Mater said, giving McQueen a friendly nudge. "She just likes me for my body."

"Doc, you really look great this morning," Sally gushed to the judge. "Did you do something different with your side-view mirrors?"

Doc Hudson sighed. "What do you want, Sally?"

"Come on," she pleaded, "make this guy fix the road. The town needs this." Sally not only acted as the town attorney, she also owned the Cosy Cone Motel. She knew that the town was dependent on the road. How would they ever get customers if no one could drive to Radiator Springs?

Doc shot McQueen an angry glance. "No. I know his type. Race car." His grille tucked into a frown. "He's the last thing this town needs."

"Fellow citizens," Sally said, turning to the cars who lined the courtroom, "you're all aware of our town's proud history. It is our job and our pleasure to take care of the travellers on our stretch of that road. How, I ask you, are we to care for travellers if there is no road for them to drive on? Luigi, what do you have at your store?"

"Tyres," the little Italian import replied.

"And if no one can get to you?" Sally prompted.

"I won't sell any tyres," Luigi replied. His front bumper dropped in horror. "I will lose everything!"

"Flo, what'll happen if no one can come to your station to buy gas?" Sally asked the cafØ owner

"I'll go out of business and we'll have to leave town!" Flo cried.

Sally turned to the revved-up crowd. "And what's going to happen to all of us if Flo leaves town and closes her station?"

Suddenly, the entire town realized that their very lives depended on that road!

"So, don't you think the car responsible should fix our road?" Sally demanded. "Oh, he can do it," she said, casting a look in McQueen's direction. "He's got the horsepower. So what do you want him to do?"

"Fix the road!" the cars shouted, rallying.

"Because we are a town worth fixing!" Sally was on a roll now.

"Order in the court!" Doc shouted. Once the courtroom was quiet, the irritated judge gave Sally a sidelong glance.

"Seems like my mind has been changed for me," Doc finally said grudgingly.

McQueen was furious. "Oh, I am so not taking you to dinner," he grumbled to Sally.

"Oh, that's okay, *Stickers*." Sally smiled, poking

fun at his sticker-covered frame. "You can take Bessie."

"Bessie," McQueen repeated. "Who's Bessie?"

"This here is Bessie," Doc said as he showed McQueen the massive piece of heavy machinery. She was steaming and dripping, and she was covered in a thick layer of tar. "Finest road-pavin' machine ever built," Doc announced. "I'm hereby sentencing you to community service. You're gonna fix the road under my supervision."

"What?" McQueen demanded, completely repulsed. "This place is crazy."

"Hey," Mater whispered, leaning over to McQueen. "I know this might be a bad time right now, but you owe me $32,000 in legal fees."

"What?" McQueen cried.

"So we're gonna hitch you up to sweet Bessie," Doc went on, "and you're gonna pull her nice."

"You gotta be kidding me!" McQueen complained.

He couldn't believe it. Did this old lemon seriously expect a flashy racing car like Lightning McQueen to haul around a piece of junk like Bessie? As far as punishments went, this was cruel and unusual. "How long is this gonna take?"

"Well," Doc said thoughtfully, "if a fella does it right, should take him about five days."

"Five days?" McQueen cried. An image of Chick chatting up the folks at Dinoco flashed through his mind. "But I should be in California schmoozing Dinoco right now!"

"Then if I were you," Doc shot back, "I'd quit yappin' and start workin'. Hook him up, Mater."

"Okey-dokey." The breakdown lorry rolled forward to attach McQueen to Bessie. But the minute he removed McQueen's wheel clamp – *zoom*!

"Freedom!" McQueen shouted loudly as he zipped away. "Woo-hoo! California, here I come!" He pressed the accelerator, shooting toward the WELCOME TO RADIATOR SPRINGS sign. But suddenly, he coughed. Then he spluttered. "No. No, no, no," McQueen cried as he slowed to a stop. "Out of gas? How can I be out of gas?"

"Boy," Sheriff said as he and Sally rolled out from behind the sign, "we ain't as dumb as you think we are."

"We siphoned your gas while you were passed out," Sally added. She could hardly hide her grin. *"Ka-chow!"*

Sheriff joined Sarge and Fillmore, who were having a quart of oil at Flo's and watching McQueen haul Bessie over the road. Red was tending to some flowers near the tyre shop while Luigi fiddled with his tyre tower.

"Red, can you move over?" old Lizzie croaked from the porch of her souvenir shop. "I want to get a look at that sexy hot rod!"

"You know, I used to be a pretty good whistler," Mater said to McQueen as the rookie racing car struggled to haul Bessie. McQueen inched along, gagging on fumes from the tar. "I can't do it now, of course," Mater went on, "on account of sometimes I get fluid built up in my engine block, but Doc said he's gonna fix it, though. He can fix about anything. That's why we made him the judge. Boy, you shoulda heard me on the song Giddy Up Oom Papa Mow-Mow'. Now, I'm not one to brag, but people come pretty far to see me get low on the mow-mow'."

Bessie let out a squirt of tar. It landed all over McQueen's lightning-bolt sticker.

"Aw, man, that's just great. My lucky sticker's all dirty," McQueen griped. "Hey!" he called to the fire engine.

Red looked up from his flowers.

"Yeah, you in the red!" McQueen went on. "I could use a little hose down. Help me wash this off."

Red darted into the fire station.

"Where's he going?" McQueen asked.

"Oh, he's just a little bit shy," Mater explained. "And he hates you for killing his flowers."

"I shouldn't have to put up with this," McQueen grumbled angrily. "I am a precision instrument of speed and aerodynamics."

Mater looked blank. "You hurt your what?"

"I'm a very famous race car!" McQueen shouted.

"You are a famous race car?" Luigi cried, brightening. "I must scream to the world my excitement from the top of someplace very high! Do you know many Ferraris?"

"No," McQueen admitted. "They race on the European circuit. I'm in the Piston Cup–"

The little Italian import was unimpressed. "Luigi follow only the Ferraris," he interrupted. Then he drove off, leaving McQueen still strapped to Bessie.

Just then, two mini vans appeared on the horizon, heading into town.

"Customers, everyone!" Sally cried. "It's been a long time; just remember what we rehearsed. You all know what to do."

The town sprang into action, taking their places in front of their shops and flipping over their OPEN signs.

"I just don't see any on-ramp anywhere," Mrs Mini Van said. She and her husband bumped awkwardly over the broken road. They were looking for the Interstate.

"I know exactly where we are," Mr Mini Van

insisted, even though he didn't.

"Hello!" Sally chirped as she raced to welcome the motorists. "Welcome to Radiator Springs, gateway to Ornament Valley, legendary for its quality service and friendly hospitality. How can we help you?"

"We don't need anything," Mr Mini Van said, "thank you very much."

"Oh, honey, ask for directions to the Interstate," Mrs Mini Van begged. Her husband ignored her.

"What you really need is the sweet taste of my home made organic fuel," Fillmore suggested.

"We're just trying to find the Interstate," Mrs Mini Van explained.

"Good to see you, soldier," barked the old jeep. "Come on by Sarge's Surplus Hut."

"I do have a map over at the Cosy Cone Motel," Sally told the couple helpfully. "And, if you do stay, we offer a free Lincoln Continental breakfast."

"I don't need a map," Mr Mini Van said stubbornly. "I have the GPS."

Flo offered them fuel. Luigi suggested that they get some new tyres. Ramone even tried to sell the lost couple a flashy new paint job.

But the travellers weren't interested. In fact, all the attention made them drive a little faster to get out of Radiator Springs.

"Come back soon, okay?" Sally called as the couple sped off. "I mean, you know where we are. Tell your friends."

"*Pssst. Pssst.*" McQueen gestured to the couple as they neared the edge of town. "Hey – I know how to get to the Interstate."

"Oh, do you?" Mrs Mini Van asked as she came to a stop.

"No," McQueen admitted, "not really, but listen. I'm Lightning McQueen, the famous race car. I'm being held here against my will and I need you to call my team so they can come rescue me and get me to California in time for me to win the Piston Cup!"

The Mini Vans exchanged nervous glances. This car sounded crazy.

"Gotta be goin' now," Mr Mini Van said quickly. "Okay, bye-bye!"

Now McQueen was desperate.

"No, no, no!" he begged. Now he really sounded

insane. But what else could he do? He didn't care if he sounded out of his mind. The thought of staying in Radiator Springs was making him crazy!

He yelled after the Mini Vans, "It's the truth! I'm telling you, you gotta help me!"

But the Mini Vans took off without checking their rear-view mirrors.

"And we'll be right back to our Hank Williams marathon after a quick Piston-Cup update," a voice announced over the radio on Lizzie's porch.

McQueen looked up. Piston-Cup update? Had anyone even noticed he was missing yet? Maybe they'd send a search party!

"Still no sign of Lightning McQueen," the announcer said.

McQueen's engine raced. They *were* looking for him! Maybe the Mini Vans would tell someone they had seen him.

"Meanwhile, Chick Hicks arrived in California and today became the first car to spend practice time on the track," the voice went on.

"Yeah, well, it's just nice to get out here before the other competitors," Chick's voice boomed over the radio's speakers. "You know, get a head start."

McQueen glowered, imagining Chick and Tex laughing together at the Dinoco tent. He imagined Chick winning the Piston Cup, getting the big endorsement deals, starring in a Hollywood movie – getting everything McQueen wanted for himself.

Well, this race car isn't about to quit now, McQueen thought, snapping out of his vision. "Mater," he said to the rusty old breakdown lorry, "let me get this straight. I can go when this road is done. That's the deal, right?"

"That's what they done did said," Mater agreed.

That was all McQueen needed to hear. "Okay. Out of my way," he growled. "I've got a road to finish." McQueen focused, the way he did before a race. Then, in a moment, he was off! He put the hammer down and zipped through his work. Bessie wobbled and splashed tar across the road, groaning as the racing car pulled her far faster than she was built to go.

A short while later, Mater burst into Doc's office. "He's done!"

"Done?" Doc grumbled. He wasn't sure whether

to be impressed or suspicious. "It's only been an hour." He followed Mater out to the street, where the rest of the town was gathered. They looked at their newly fixed' road. It was a disaster.

"I'm done," McQueen panted heavily. "Look, I'm finished. Just say thank you," he said to Sally, "and I'll be on my way. That's all you gotta say."

"Whee-hoo!" Mater called as he drove to the opposite end of the road. "I'm the first one on the new road!" He drove over the bumpy splattered asphalt. "A-h-h-a-h!" he said as he was jostled back and forth. "It rides pre-etty smo-ooo-ooth."

Sally cut to the chase. "It looks awful."

McQueen glared at her. "Now it matches the rest of the town," he shot back.

Red, the shy fire engine, was so hurt by McQueen's comment that he drove off into the woods, knocking over Luigi's tower of tyres. The whole town could hear Red sobbing.

Furious, Sally wheeled to face McQueen. "Who do you think you are?" she demanded.

"Look, Doc said when I finished, I could go," McQueen said in frustration. "That was the deal."

"The deal was you fix the road, not make it worse," Doc snapped as he drove up. "Now, scrape it off; start over again."

"Hey, look, grandpa," McQueen said rudely. "I'm not a bulldozer, I'm a race car."

"Is that right?" Doc replied, clearly unimpressed. "Then why don't we just have a little race? Me and you."

McQueen cracked up. "Ho, ho, ho. Me and you," he said, unbelieving. "Is that a joke?"

"If you win, you go and I fix the road," Doc suggested. "If I win, you do the road *my* way."

McQueen couldn't believe his luck! *This car probably does zero to 60 in about three-point-five years*, he thought. *I'll run the race and be out of here in half an hour.* It was an offer he couldn't refuse.

"You know what, old-timer?" McQueen said. "That's a wonderful idea. Let's race."

"**G**entlemen, this will be a one-lap race," Sheriff announced as the whole town assembled at Willys Butte to watch the action. "You will drive to Willys Butte, go around Willys Butte and come back. There will be no bumpin', no cheatin', no spittin', no bitin', no road rage, no maimin', no oil slickin', no pushin', no shovin', no backstabbin', no road-hoggin' and no lollygaggin'."

McQueen was hardly listening. "Speed," he said to himself. "I am speed."

"Gentlemen," announced Sheriff, "start your engines."

Doc's engine turned over slowly, coughing and spluttering. With a smug laugh, McQueen started his own engine. It roared dangerously.

"Great idea, Doc," Sally muttered to herself.

"Now the road will never get done."

Luigi dropped the flag, and McQueen took off like a rocket. The town cheered as he sent up a cloud of dust behind his rear tyres. But when the dust cleared, everyone saw that Doc was still standing at the starting line!

"Doc, the flag means 'go'," Luigi explained.

Doc didn't move.

"Uh, Doc?" Ramone said slowly. "What are you doing, man?"

"Oh, dear," Doc said in a flat voice. "It would seem I'm off to a poor start. Well, better late than never." He turned to the rusty breakdown lorry. "Come on, Mater. You got your tow cable?"

"Well, yeah," Mater said as he and Doc rolled along the track, far behind McQueen. "I always got my tow cable. Why?"

"Oh," Doc said, "just in case."

Curious, the other cars followed Doc and Mater.

McQueen was flying along the road, showing off his incredible speed. "I am speed," he said to himself, taking the turn as he rounded the turn on the dirt track. "Nothing can stop me now.

I'm halfway to California–"

Whoa! The turn was tight and, before he could register what was happening, McQueen had lost control, dropping off a low cliff and landing hard in the sand below.

"Ooh, man!" Ramone said, wincing at the sight of McQueen. The racing car was wedged in a grove of sharp cacti. "Ow!"

"Whoa . . . " Fillmore agreed. "Bad trip, man."

McQueen revved his engine, but it was no use. He couldn't move.

Mater giggled.

"You drive like you fix roads . . . " Doc said as McQueen spun his wheels, ". . . lousy." The judge turned to the breakdown lorry. "Have fun fishing, Mater."

As Doc drove away, Mater cast down his tow cable and dragged McQueen up the hill by his rear axle. "I'm startin' to think he knowed you was gonna crash," Mater said to the racing car.

"Thank you, Mater," McQueen said gratefully as the lorry pulled him back onto the track.

Radiator Springs was turning out to be harder to leave than he'd ever expected.

"I can make a little turn on dirt, you think? No!" McQueen grumbled late that night as he scraped off the asphalt he had poured over the broken road. "And now I'm a day behind. I'm never gonna get out of here."

"Hey," Ramone called as McQueen muttered to himself, "you need a new paint job, man."

"No, thank you," McQueen said automatically. He didn't have time for a new paint job; he needed to fix that road! He couldn't believe he had lost a race to an old grandpa car!

"How about some organic fuel?" Fillmore suggested hopefully.

McQueen sighed. "Pass."

"Whoo!" Flo said, eyeing McQueen. "Watchin' him work is makin' me thirsty. Anybody else want something to drink?"

"Nah, not me, Flo," Mater said. "I'm on one of them there special diets. I'm a pre-sisional instrument of speed and aero-matics."

McQueen grumbled on. " You race like you fix roads'," he mimicked, mocking Doc's insult. "I'll show him. I will show him." He grunted, throwing himself into his work. Soon he had finished the scraping. He hooked himself up to Bessie and started repaving.

Splat!

"Aww, great!" McQueen shouted as he tried to shake off the tar Bessie had squirted all over him. "I hate it, hate, hate, hate, hate it!"

But no matter how much he hated it, McQueen kept on working all through the night.

"Whee-hee!" Mater shouted the next morning as dawn broke over Radiator Springs. "Whee-hoo!"

Hearing the whoops and hollers, Sally drove out of her motel to investigate. She found Mater turning circles and spinning happily on a beautiful newly paved stretch of road. She gasped.

Wow, she thought. McQueen had done an amazing job!

"Morning, Sally," Mater called. "Hey, look at this here fancy new road that Lightning McQueen done just made!"

Soon the other cars had gathered on the road. Ramone bounced on his hydraulics, getting as low as he could go.

"*Oooh, Ramone,*" Flo cooed to her husband "Mama ain't seen you that low in years."

"I haven't seen a road like this in years," Ramone replied.

"Well, then," Flo said playfully, "let's cruise, baby."

Soon all the cars were out taking a spin on the sleek new road.

"*E bellissima!*" Luigi cried as he gawked at the road from the front of his shop. "It's like it was paved by angels!"

"Doc, look at this," Sally said as the gruff old roadster pulled up to the fresh asphalt. "Shoulda tossed him into the cactus a lot sooner, huh?"

Doc grunted. "Well, he ain't finished yet. He's still got a long way to go."

"Hey, Luigi!" Lizzie called as she rolled past the tyre shop. "This new road makes your place look like a dump!"

"Ah, the crazy old devil woman–" Luigi said grouchily. But, as he looked up at his shop, he gasped. "She's-a right!"

Doc peered down at the road, inspecting the work closely. "Huh – that punk actually did a good job," he muttered. "Well, now, where the heck is he?" Looking around, he noticed Bessie sitting by the side of the road. McQueen was nowhere in sight.

Just then, Doc heard the sound of a racing-car engine in the distance. He sped off after the noise.

"Sheriff," Doc said as he drove up to the cliff edge at Willys Butte, "is he making another run for it?"

Sheriff chuckled. "No, no," he explained, "he ran out of asphalt in the middle of the night and asked me if he could come down here. All he's trying to do is make that there turn."

Sure enough, McQueen was rounding the same turn that had made him crash the day before. Just as he reached it, his tyres skidded and he swerved, then crashed. "No, no, no, no!" McQueen cried as he drove back to try again. "Ahh, great! I've done perfect turns on every track I've ever raced on."

"Huh," Doc said as he watched McQueen try to take the curve over and over. He smiled a little at the racing car's determination. "Sheriff, why don't you go get yourself a quart of oil at Flo's?" the judge suggested. "I'll keep an eye on him."

"Well, thanks, Doc," Sheriff said in surprise.

"I've been feelin' a quart low." He drove off, leaving Doc to deal with McQueen.

Doc watched carefully as McQueen tried the turn again. Sure enough, he crashed again and came to a stop, spitting dirt from his grille.

Finally, the old car decided to help out McQueen. "This ain't asphalt, son," Doc explained simply as he rolled up to the racing car. "This is dirt."

"Oh, great," McQueen snapped. "So you're a judge, a doctor and a racing expert?"

"I'll put it simple," Doc said patiently. "If you're going hard enough left, you'll find yourself turning right."

"Oh, right," McQueen said, his voice dripping with sarcasm. "That makes perfect sense. Turn right to go left. Thank you. Or should I say no, thank you'," he went on, his voice rising in frustration, "because in Opposite World, maybe that really means thank you." *What does that old car know about racing, anyway?* McQueen thought as he sped off along the track, throwing plumes of dust all over Doc.

Once the dust cleared, McQueen saw that Doc

had driven away. Suddenly, he began to wonder if Doc's advice might work. *Well, I might as well try it*, he thought. *Nothing else seems to be helping.*

McQueen sped toward the turn. "Turn right to go left," he said to himself. It didn't make any sense.

At the last moment, McQueen turned sharply right – and shot straight over the cliff.

"Ooh," he cried as he landed right back in the cacti. "Oh, that hurt."

12

"Turn right to go left," McQueen muttered later that afternoon as he pulled Bessie down the road. He was filthy and covered with cactus thorns. "Guess what? I tried it, and you know what? This crazy thing happened – I went right!"

"You keep talking to yourself, people'll think you're crazy," Lizzie said.

"Thanks for the tip," McQueen told the forgetful old car.

Lizzie glared at the racing car. "I wasn't talking to you!"

Meanwhile, McQueen's gorgeous new road had inspired the townsfolk to spruce up their shops. Mater was using his cable to straighten his TOW MATER sign. Ramone was repainting a fence as Flo looked on, clearly impressed. Red was busy washing the leaning tower of tyres.

Che bellissimo!" Sally cried as she watched Luigi's assistant, Guido, paint the tyre shop while Luigi cleaned the windows. "It looks great!" She was thrilled to see the townspeople taking pride in Radiator Springs. *Actually*, she thought, *there's only one car who still needs a makeover. . . .* She looked over at the filthy racing car, who was muttering to himself as he paved.

"While I'm stuck here paving this stinking road," he griped, "Chick's in California schmoozing Dinoco." McQueen pulled harder, working out his anger. "*My* Dinoco. Whoa, whoa, whoa!" he said, stopping to straighten up. "Who's touching me?"

"You have a slow leak," Luigi explained as Guido checked the air in McQueen's tyres. Cactus prickles stuck out of the rubber like porcupine quills.

"Guido," Luigi said, motioning to his assistant, who held a can of tyre sealant, "he fix. You make-a such-a nice new road. You come to my shop. Luigi take-a good care of you – even though you not a Ferrari. You buy four tyres, I give you a full-size spare absolutely free." He smiled enthusiastically.

McQueen sighed. He was in a terrible mood. "Look," he said irritably, "I get all my tyres for free." *Don t these people know anything about famous racing cars*? he wondered.

Just as Luigi drove off, McQueen was blasted with cold water. "Ohh!" he screamed. "Stop!"

The water stopped, and McQueen found himself facing Red. Sally was standing beside him.

"Ooh, Red," Sally said, "you missed a spot. See it right there? Right on the hood? Right there."

"No, no–" McQueen cried as Red blasted the remaining piece of cactus on his hood. "Ah . . . stop!" he spluttered. "Ah, that's cold! Whoo! Help! Please! Stop!"

Red kept blasting water at McQueen until the cactus flew off.

"Thanks, Red," Sally said.

"What was that for?" McQueen demanded, coughing and blinking.

"Do you want to stay at the Cosy Cone, or what?" Sally asked bluntly. "I mean, if you do, you gotta be clean."

"What?" McQueen was really confused now. "I don't get it—"

"Nothing," Sally said, trying to sound as if it was no big deal. "I just thought I'd say thank you for doing a great job by letting you stay at the Cosy Cone."

McQueen was shocked. "Wait, you're being nice to me."

"I mean, if you want to stay at the dirty impound, that's fine," Sally went on. "You know, I understand – you criminal types."

"No, no, no, no – that's okay." McQueen looked in admiration at the motel in the distance. It was much nicer than the impound, that was for sure. "Yeah, the Cosy Cone."

"Cone number one, if you want." Sally drove off, accidentally running into a pile of orange cones. They all fell over. Embarrassed, she drove quickly into her motel office.

Just then, Mater appeared. He pulled up beside McQueen and began chattering away. "You know, I once knew this girl Doreen. Good-lookin' girl. Looked just like a Jaguar, only she was a truck. You know, I used to crash into her just so I could spoke to her." Mater grinned proudly.

"What are you talking about?" McQueen asked.

"I dunno," Mater admitted. "Hey, I know somethin' we can do tonight, 'cause I'm in charge of watchin' ya."

"No, Mater, I gotta finish this road and I have to get out of here."

"Well, that's all right, Mr I-Can't-Turn-on-Dirt." Mater started to drive off. "You probably couldn't handle it, anyway."

"Whoa, whoa, easy now, Mater," McQueen said indignantly. "You know who you're talking to? This is Lightning McQueen. I can handle anything."

Later that night, McQueen found himself looking at a herd of sleeping tractors. "Mater," he said, "I'm not doing this."

"Oh, c'mon," Mater urged, "you'll love it! Tractor tipping's fun! When I say go, we go. But don't let Frank catch you. Go!" Mater took off.

"Whoa!" McQueen cried. "Wha-who-who-who's Frank?" He raced after the breakdown lorry. "Mater. Wait, Mater!"

"'kay, here's what you do," Mater explained, as he arrived at the bottom of the hill where the tractors stood sleeping. "You just sneak up in front of 'em and then honk, and they do the rest. Watch this." Slowly and quietly, Mater drove up to a tractor.

Honk!

The tractor woke up, startled. It let out a low

moan as it very slowly started tipping over. A puff of smoke burst from its exhaust pipe.

Mater chuckled. "I swear, tractors are so dumb!" he cried gleefully. He sneaked up on another one and honked, then laughed as it tipped over. "I don't care who you are, that's funny right there. Oh, your turn, bud!"

"Mater, I can't," McQueen said. "I don't even have a horn."

"Baby!" Mater teased. Then he started imitating a chicken. "Bwak, bock, bock, bock!"

"Fine, stop, stop, okay?" McQueen sighed. "All right. I'll do something." He drove up to a sleeping tractor and revved his engine.

The roar was so loud that the whole field of tractors woke up! With a group moan, they all tipped over.

McQueen and Mater laughed.

Suddenly, with a strange whine, a giant combine harvester appeared. Blades whirling, he lunged at them like an angry bull.

"That's Frank!" Mater shouted, whipping around.

McQueen sped off after the breakdown lorry.

"Run! Run!" Mater hollered, laughing his bumper off. "Old Frank's gonna catch you! Run! He's gonna get you!"

McQueen didn't know why Mater was laughing; that combine harvester was big and angry! Frank closed in behind them as they tore toward an opening in the fence. They made it through the hole just in time and raced onto the open road as fast as their wheels could carry them.

"I haven't seen Frank that excited about somethin' since the last time he was excited about somethin'," Mater said as he and McQueen made their way back to town. "Must've been your red bumper. Tomorrow night we can go and look for the ghost light."

"I can't wait, Mater," McQueen said sarcastically.

"Oh, boy, you gotta admit that was fu-un," Mater said happily. "Well, we better get you back to the impound lot."

"Um, you know," McQueen said awkwardly, "actually, Sally's gonna let me stay at the motel."

"Oh . . . getting cosy at the Cone, is we?" Mater teased, arriving at the motel's parking lot.

"You're in love with Miss Sally."

"No, I'm not," McQueen said. "No way."

"*Way*. You're in love with Miss Sally." Mater turned his teasing into a song. "You're in love with Miss Sally!" The lorry turned around and started driving backwards, taunting the racing car. "You love 'er, you love 'er, you love 'er, you love 'er–"

"Will you stop that?" McQueen said.

"Stop what?" Mater asked.

"That driving backwards stuff," McQueen said with a shudder. "It's creepin' me out. You're going to wreck or something."

"Wreck? Shoot, I'm the world's best backwards driver. You just watch this right here, lover boy." With a whoop, Mater sped backwards and wove between the Cosy Cone's traffic-cone guest rooms. He came close to them but didn't knock over a single one.

"What are you doing?" McQueen shouted as Mater swerved back and forth. "Watch out! Look out! Mater, stop showing off now, okay? Hey, take it easy, Mater! Look out!"

Mater hooted as he drove off between a few trees

and shrubs. "Ain't no need to watch where I'm going," he bragged as he headed towards McQueen at top speed. Just as he and McQueen were about to collide, Mater spun around and came to a full stop, facing the shocked racing car. "Just need to know where I been!"

"Whoa!" McQueen said, truly impressed. "That was incredible." He laughed out loud. "How'd you do that?"

"Rear-view mirrors," Mater said simply. "We'll get you some, and I'll teach you if you want."

"Yeah," McQueen said thoughtfully, "maybe I'll use it in my big race."

"What's so important about this race of yours, anyway?" Mater asked.

"It's not just a race." McQueen suddenly became serious as he explained. "We're talking about the Piston Cup. I've been dreaming about it my whole life. I'll be the first rookie in history ever to win it and, when I do, we're talking big new sponsor with private helicopters; no more medicated bumper ointment, no more rusty old cars–"

"What's wrong with rusty old cars?" Mater

asked, sounding hurt. After all, he himself was rusty and old.

"Well, I don't mean you, Mater," McQueen said, realizing his mistake. He hadn't meant to hurt Mater's feelings. "I mean *other* old cars. You know, not like you. I like you."

"It's okay, buddy," Mater said. "Hey, you think maybe one day I could get a ride in one of them helicopters? I mean, I've always wanted to ride in one of them fancy helicopters."

"Yeah, yeah," McQueen said casually. "Yeah, sure, sure."

"You mean it?" Mater's engine hummed in excitement.

"Oh, yeah," McQueen promised. "Anything you say."

Mater's smile disappeared, and his expression turned serious. "I knew it! I knowed I made a good choice."

"In what?" McQueen asked.

"My best friend," Mater said simply. McQueen smiled. Then Mater spun his tow cable like a helicopter propeller and sped away backwards, flashing his one good headlight. "See you tomorrow, buddy!" he called. "McQueen and Sally, parked beneath a tree, K-I-S-sumpin', sumpin', sumpin' . . . T," he sang as he drove away.

McQueen couldn't help laughing as Mater's voice faded into the distance. Finally, he turned and started looking for his cone.

"Number one . . . " he muttered as he searched. "Number one . . . " He found it. The racing car drove inside and looked around. "Ah, this is nice–"

"Hey, Stickers!" Sally said, appearing outside the cone. "I overheard you talking to Mater."

McQueen was horrified. Had she overheard Mater teasing him about having a crush on her? He hoped not.

"When? You just – just now? What did – what did you hear?" he asked nervously.

"Oh, just something about a helicopter ride," Sally said.

"Oh, yeah, yeah," McQueen said, half to himself. "He got a kick out of that, didn't he?"

"Did you mean it?" Sally asked. "You'll get him a ride?"

"Oh," McQueen said absently. "Who knows? I mean, first things first. I gotta get outta here and make the race."

"You know," Sally said, "Mater trusts you."

McQueen thought about that for a moment. He hadn't really taken his promise to Mater seriously, but Mater *would* take it seriously. "Yeah, okay."

"Did you mean that?" Sally pressed.

"Look, I'm exhausted," McQueen said, not knowing what else to say. Then he added, "It's kinda been a long day."

"Yeah, okay," Sally said. "Night."

"Hey," McQueen called as she started to drive away. "You know, thanks for letting me stay here. It's nice to be out of the impound. And this is . . . it's great. Newly refurbished, right?"

Sally smiled. "Yeah." She was proud of her motel – and McQueen had just given her a real compliment. *Maybe there's some good in him after all*, she thought. "Good night."

McQueen moaned. He was having a terrible nightmare. It was the Piston Cup final, and he was being beaten – by Frank the combine harvester! In a whirlwind, Frank took the trophy and the Dinoco sponsorship and had gorgeous female cars fawning all over him. It was horrible.

"No!" McQueen cried, jerking awake. He looked at the alarm clock. A tiny car had just popped out of a cone and honked its horn. "I gotta get out of here."

McQueen sped off to find Sheriff. He needed his daily fuel ration. But Sheriff wasn't at the impound, so McQueen zipped over to Doc Hudson's office.

"Hey, have you seen Sheriff?" McQueen asked as he burst into the office. He realized with a sudden start that Sheriff was up on a hydraulic lift, getting a private smog check. His entire underside was exposed! *"Ahh!"* McQueen cried in horror. "Oh my gosh."

"Hey, what are you doin'?" Doc Hudson demanded. "Wait for him at Flo's. Now, get out of here."

"I've been trying to get out of here for three days!" McQueen shot back.

"Hope you enjoyed the show!" Sheriff called as McQueen drove off.

On his way out, the frustrated racing car kicked an old oil can into Doc's garage. He cringed as something crashed inside. *Oops.* He hadn't meant to break anything. In spite of the signs that read NO TRESPASSING and PRIVATE PROPERTY, McQueen decided he'd better go inside and make sure everything was okay.

"Whoa, Doc," McQueen said as he drove cautiously into the office, "time to clean out the garage, buddy." He scanned the junk littering the garage; the place was piled high with mess. As he headed towards the back of the office, he spotted something on Doc's desk. It was covered in dirt and filled with tools, but the shape was familiar. McQueen rolled over for a better look. He gasped at what he saw. It was a racing trophy. But not just any trophy – it was the Piston Cup!

THE HUDSON HORNET, it read, CHAMPION: 1951.

"He has a Piston Cup?" McQueen whispered, stunned. On the floor nearby were two more, from 1952 and 1953. "Oh my gosh, *three* Piston Cups?" He couldn't believe it. But sure enough, he came across a newspaper article proclaiming Doc "Champion for All Time."

"The sign says 'stay out'," Doc growled as he appeared in the doorway.

"Y-you have three Piston Cups!" McQueen stammered. "You're the Hudson Hornet!"

"Wait over at Flo's," Doc snapped angrily, "like I told you."

McQueen started to leave but, in the doorway, he stopped in his tracks. "Of course!" he said, realizing the truth. "I-I can't believe I didn't see it before. You're the Fabulous Hudson Hornet. You still hold the record for most wins in a single season. Oh, we gotta talk. You gotta show me your tricks, please–"

"I already tried that," Doc pointed out.

"I mean, you won the championship three times!" McQueen gushed. "Look at those trophies!"

"You look." Doc fixed McQueen with a steady gaze. "All I see is a bunch of empty cups." With that, he slammed the door in McQueen's face.

15

McQueen just couldn't keep news like that to himself. He knew that most of the townsfolk would be gathered at the cafØ, so he zipped over there at top speed. "Oh my gosh!" he said as he drove into Flo's. "Guys! Did you know Doc is a famous race car?"

For a moment, everyone was silent.

Then they burst out laughing.

"Doc?" Sheriff cried. "Our Doc?"

"Not Doc Hudson?" Sarge bellowed.

"Did you hear that one?" Ramone – radiant in new yellow paint – was laughing hysterically. "He's saying Doc's a . . .this guy cracks me up!"

"No, no, no," McQueen insisted. He felt almost desperate. He had to convince them of who Doc was. "It's true! He's a real racing legend. He's the

Fabulous Hudson Hornet!"

"Fabulous?" Flo said doubtfully. "I've never seen Doc drive more than 20 miles an hour. I mean, have you ever seen him race?"

"No," McQueen admitted, "but I wish I could've." McQueen was dead serious. "They say he was amazing. He won three Piston Cups!"

Mater spat out the oil he'd been drinking. "He did what in his cup?"

McQueen tried to persuade them that Doc Hudson was the real deal, but the townsfolk didn't buy it.

"I think the heat's startin' to get to the boy," Sheriff said.

"Are you sick, buddy?" Mater asked.

Sally hit the fuel lever with her tyre. *Ding ding ding*! She filled up McQueen's tank.

"Hey! Hey!" Sheriff protested. This could be dangerous. "What're you doing?"

"It's okay, Sheriff," Sally said. "You can trust me, right?"

"I trust you, all right," Sheriff said, narrowing his eyes at McQueen. "It's him I'm worried about."

"I trust him," Sally said. "C'mon," she told McQueen. "Let's take a drive."

Once his tank was full, McQueen considered heading for the open road. Nothing was stopping him now.

Sally started toward a mountain in the distance. "Hey, Stickers," she called. "You comin' or what?" She drove away, letting McQueen decide for himself whether or not to make a run for it.

After hesitating for just a moment, he sped after Sally.

"*Mmm-hmm*," Flo said knowingly to Sheriff. "And you thought he was gonna run."

"Okay," McQueen said when he caught up with Sally, "you got me out here. Where are we going?"

"I don't know." Sally zipped off.

McQueen was surprised by how fast Sally was as he chased her into a forest. Playfully, she splashed him with an icy puddle, and the shock took his breath away. Grinning, Sally tried to splash him again, but McQueen dodged the water – and ran into a puddle of mud.

Sally laughed as McQueen zoomed after her. He accidentally drove into a pile of leaves, which stuck to his muddy surface.

As they rounded a few turns, McQueen took the lead, but Sally shot past him again. The two cars passed through a rock tunnel as the road wound up the mountain. McQueen was starting to notice the natural beauty that surrounded him.

As he took a curve, McQueen caught sight of Sally passing a majestic waterfall up ahead. He was stunned by how beautiful she looked. He smiled at her and she laughed. His grille was covered in insects!

McQueen spat the insects out and sped after her again. Soon he found himself at the top of the mountain. Sally had stopped in front of an old abandoned hotel.

"Wow," McQueen said as he looked around at the dusty hotel. "What is this place?"

Sally sighed. "Wheel Well. Used to be the most popular stop on the Mother Road." She was referring to the old Highway 66.

McQueen looked carefully at Sally and wondered. She was a brand-new Porsche. A fancy car. Why was she living in the little town of Radiator Springs in the middle of nowhere?

"How does a Porsche wind up in a place like this?" he asked, marvelling.

"Well, it's really pretty simple," Sally told him. "I was an attorney in L.A., living life in the fast lane. And you know what? It never felt . . . happy."

"Yeah . . ." McQueen said thoughtfully, then caught himself. "I mean, really?"

"Yeah," Sally went on. "So I left California – just drove and drove and finally broke down right here. Doc fixed me up. Flo took me in. Well, they all did. And I never left."

McQueen thought for a moment. He had to admit, his time in Radiator Springs hadn't been all bad. Still, he couldn't really imagine himself living there. "I understand you need to recharge the old batteries, but you know, after a while, why didn't you go back?"

"I fell in love," Sally said simply.

McQueen's tyres deflated a little. "Corvette?"

"No." Sally drove to the edge of the cliff. "I fell in love . . . with this."

McQueen followed her and looked down. "Whoa." Below them, Radiator Springs was a glistening green oasis at the base of a towering mountain range. The setting sun made the breathtaking waterfall sparkle in the distance. Beyond Radiator Springs, cars zipped by on the Interstate, oblivious to the beautiful scene. "Look at that," McQueen said to himself. "They're driving right by. They don't even know what they're missing."

"Forty years ago," Sally said, "that Interstate down there didn't exist. Back then, cars came across the country a whole different way."

"How do you mean?" McQueen asked.

"Well, the road didn't cut through the land like that Interstate," Sally explained. "It moved with the land; you know it rose, it fell, it curved. Cars didn't drive on it to make great time. They drove on it to *have* a great time."

McQueen was quiet. His whole life was about speed. The idea of driving slowly, for fun, was strange. "What happened?"

"The town got bypassed just to save ten minutes of driving," Sally said.

McQueen imagined what the Wheel Well and Radiator Springs must have been like when they were thriving. "How great would it have been to see this place in its heyday?"

"Oh," Sally said in a soft, sincere voice, "I can't tell you how many times I've dreamed of that. But one of these days we'll find a way to get it back on the map."

"Hey, listen," McQueen said thoughtfully, "thanks for the drive. I had a great time. It's kind of nice to slow down every once in a while."

"You're welcome," Sally said, smiling.

The two cars headed back to town in silence, enjoying the view.

When they got back to town, Mater pulled up alongside McQueen.

"Hey, hey," Mater whispered, "if anyone asks you, we were out smashin' mailboxes, okay?" The breakdown lorry tore off.

Just then, McQueen heard a noise. The ground was vibrating. And something was . . . mooing?

It was a tractor stampede – and it was heading straight for him!

McQueen got out of the tractors' way just in time. The stampede rolled into town, where Ramone was busy painting the white divider line down the newest stretch of asphalt.

"Oh, man," Ramone groaned as he scurried away, "the paint's still wet!"

Red was watering his flowers at the base of the

Stanley statue. As the tractors drew near, he steeled himself to face the beasts. There was no way he was going to let a bunch of tractors take out his newly replanted posies!

The fire engine unleashed a mighty blast and the tractors stopped in their tracks. With a group moo, they tipped over, except for a few strays who scattered in different directions.

"No, no, no, get out of the store!" Luigi cried frantically as his tyre shop was overrun by stray tractors. "Hey! Don't eat the radial! Here, take the snow tyre!"

"Mater!" Sheriff bellowed.

"I wasn't tractor tippin'!" Mater insisted.

"Then where did all of these gol' dern tractors come from?" Sheriff demanded.

McQueen stood at the edge of town, smiling at the crazy tractors. Suddenly, he noticed one heading out of town. "Hey, guys?" he called. "There's one going this way. I got it!" He headed off to herd the tractor, following it all the way to Willys Butte. McQueen whistled. "Come here, come here, tractor." He followed it to the edge of the rise that overlooked the flat-topped hill. "Don't wander off." Catching sight of a lone car, McQueen grew quiet. It was Doc. "What are you doing with those old racing tyres?" McQueen muttered to himself. He sneaked behind some brush to see what Doc was going to do.

Down below, Doc rubbed the dirt with a tyre and sighed.

"Come on, Doc," McQueen whispered, eager to see the Hornet in action. "Drive."

Doc got into position, focusing on the track ahead. He took a moment to blow the carbon out of his pipes, then took off.

"Whoa!" McQueen said as Doc ripped down the track, kicking up plumes of dust behind him. McQueen watched nervously as Doc charged the turn at full speed, but the old car countersteered, taking the curve beautifully. Finally, Doc finished the course and skidded to a stop in the same place he'd started. He was out of breath but smiling.

"Wow," McQueen said, driving up to Doc. "You're amazing!"

Doc's expression hardened. He hadn't realized that anyone was watching. Without a word, the old racing car took off, throwing dirt into McQueen's grille.

"What are you doing?" McQueen coughed. He wasn't about to let Doc leave without a word. "Doc, wait!" The racing car followed Doc back into town.

Doc rumbled into his office, slamming the door behind him, but McQueen caught it with a tyre and forced his way in. "Doc, hold it. Seriously, your driving's incredible."

"Wonderful," Doc grumbled. "Now, go away."

"Hey, I mean it," McQueen insisted. "You've still got it!"

Doc glared at the young racing car. "I'm asking you to leave."

"C'mon," McQueen begged. "I'm a race car. You're a much older race car, but under the hood, you and I are the same."

"We are not the same!" Doc bellowed, losing his usual cool. "Understand? Now, get out!" Doc drove to the door and held it open.

But McQueen didn't budge. "How could a car like you quit at the top of your game?"

"You think I quit?" Doc demanded. He yanked

a chain, clicking on an overhead light. Below it was a framed article. CRASH WIPES OUT HUDSON HORNET, the headline read, above a photo of a much younger Doc – wrecked on a racetrack infield.

"Right . . . " McQueen said slowly as his racing history came back to him, "your big wreck in '54."

"They quit on *me*." Doc was silent for a moment. "When I finally got put together, I went back expecting a big welcome. You know what they said? 'You're history.' Moved right on to the next rookie standing in line." He looked carefully at the photograph. "There was a lot left in me. I never got a chance to show 'em. I keep that to remind me never to go back. I just never expected that that world would find me here."

"Hey, look, Doc," McQueen said, an edge in his voice, "I'm not them."

"Oh, yeah?" Doc demanded. "When is the last time you cared about something except yourself, hot rod? You name me one time, and I will take it all back."

McQueen hesitated. As much as he wanted to show the older car that he was wrong, he couldn't come up with anything that would convince Doc – or himself – otherwise.

"*Uh-huh*," Doc said. "I didn't think so. These are good folk around here who care about one another. I don't want them depending on someone they can't count on."

"Count on?" McQueen said. "You've been here how long and your friends don't even know who you are. Who's caring only about himself?"

"Just finish that road and get outta here," Doc said. He drove off, leaving McQueen alone with his thoughts.

17

As the sun peeked over the mountains the next morning, Mater yawned, stretched and drove out to the edge of the new road. Doc drove up next to him and the two autos surveyed the road. It reached into the horizon, as flat and even as a field of fresh snow.

"He's done," Mater said quietly. "He musta finished it while we were all sleepin'."

"Good riddance," Doc grumbled. As he drove away, he passed the rest of the townsfolk, who were gazing sadly at the road, thinking McQueen was gone.

"He's gone?" Flo asked.

"Well," Sarge said, trying to rally his friends and keep up a brave face, "we wouldn't want him to miss that race of his."

"Oh, dude," Ramone said to Sheriff, whose eyes were sparkling, "are you crying?"

"What?" Sheriff *was* crying, but he didn't want the others to see what a big softy he was. "No, no, no!" he insisted. "I'm happy. I don't have to watch him every second of the day any more. I'm glad he's gone."

Red burst into tears and drove away, knocking over Luigi's stack of tyres – again.

"What's wrong with Red?" a voice asked. It was McQueen.

"Oh, he's just sad 'cause you left town," Mater explained, "and went to your big race to win the Piston Cup that you've always dreamed about your whole life and get that big ol' sponsor and that fancy helicopter you were talkin' about–"

"Lightning! There you are!" The townsfolk gathered around the racing car, chattering happily.

"Wait a minute!" Mater said, the truth finally dawning on him. "*Aw*, I knew you wouldn't leave without saying goodbye." He gave McQueen a friendly punch with his tyre.

"What are you doing here, son?" Sheriff

demanded. "You're gonna miss your race. Now, don't worry, I'll give you a police escort, and we'll make up the time."

"Thank you, Sheriff," McQueen said gratefully. "Well, you know, I can't go just yet." He smiled playfully.

The townsfolk looked at one another in confusion.

"Why not?" Sheriff asked.

"I'm not sure these tyres can get me all the way to California," McQueen replied, glancing at Luigi and Guido.

"Pit stop?" Guido asked hopefully.

"Yeah," McQueen said. "Does anybody know what time Luigi's opens?"

"Oh-ho-ho!" Luigi said, laughing. "I can't believe it!" He quickly flipped over his CLOSED sign to read OPEN, and the two Italian cars rolled aside so that McQueen could come into their garage for a complete overhaul. "Four new tyres?" Luigi cried, thrilled. "*Grazie,* Mr Lightning, *grazie.*"

"Would you look at that?" Flo said as the townsfolk peered at McQueen through Luigi's freshly cleaned window.

"Our first real customer in years!" Luigi said as he secured McQueen in a lift. "I am filled with-a tears of ecstasy, for this is a most glorious day of my life."

"All right, Luigi, give me the best set of black-walls you got," McQueen ordered.

The lift dropped sharply down. "No, no, no, no," Luigi said as he made his way to a special curtained-off section of the shop. "You don't-a know what you want. Black-wall tyres, they blend into the pavement, but these–" He whipped back the curtain. "White-wall tyres – they say, Look at me! Here I am! *Loooove* me!'"

"All right," McQueen said mildly, "you're the expert. Oh, and don't forget the spare." And with that, Luigi and Guido got to work.

"Uh-huh-huh?" Luigi said with a grin as McQueen admired his new white-walls in a three-way mirror. "What did Luigi tell you, eh?"

"Wow, you were right," McQueen admitted, smiling at his flashy new tyres. "Better than a Ferrari, huh?"

Luigi's smile evaporated. "Eh, no."

McQueen decided he'd better check out all the shops in town. "Wow," he said as he tasted some of Fillmore's organic fuel. "This organic fuel is great! Why haven't I heard about it before?"

"It's a conspiracy, man!" Fillmore shouted. "The oil companies got a grip on the government. They're feeding us a bunch of lies, man!"

"Okay," McQueen said slowly. "I'll take a case!"

Next, he went to Sarge's Surplus Hut and picked out some night-vision goggles for his drive to California. Then he chose a few Radiator-Springs bumper stickers from Lizzie's memorabilia shop. At Ramone's, he got a snazzy new paint job – with a brand-new lightning-bolt design. "Yeah!" McQueen said, laughing as he looked at the fresh paint. "*Ka-chow!*"

When Sally saw McQueen later that day, she couldn't believe his makeover. He was sparkling and detailed to perfection.

"*Ka-pow!*" McQueen said, showing off his new look. "What do you think? Radiator Springs looks pretty good on me."

Sally laughed. "I'll say!" She checked out his

new paint job. "*Ka-chow!*" she said admiringly.

"You're gonna fit right in, in California," she continued, looking at him all the while.

Suddenly, Sally realized something. "Oh my goodness, it looks like you've helped everybody in town."

"Yeah, everybody except one, " McQueen said, cueing the town to light up their signs. One by one, the lights flickered on.

"They fixed their neon," Sally said quietly, taking in the beauty of the town.

"Just like in its heyday, right?" McQueen said.

Sally sighed. "It's even better than I pictured it. Thank you."

Just then, Flo pulled onto the brand-new street. "Low and slow?" she said to Ramone.

"Oh, yeah," he agreed and, next moment, he and his wife were cruising down the strip. The two cars snuggled close, happier than they had been in years.

McQueen tried to take Sally for a cruise, but Lizzie stole him away.

"Lizzie!" Sally said in protest.

Mater was right there. "Miss Sally, may I have

this cruise?" he asked.

Sally smiled. "Of course."

McQueen tried to dodge away from Lizzie, but she wouldn't let him escape her.

"I remember when Stanley first asked me to take a drive with him," she said, reminiscing.

McQueen was wondering how he could get to Sally when Mater towed him away. Lizzie happily continued to talk to herself.

"Hey!" McQueen said as he finally found himself next to Sally.

"Thanks, Mater," Sally said to the breakdown lorry.

"Good evenin', you two." Mater gave Sally a broad wink, then drove off backwards.

Just as McQueen and Sally were about to start cruising, Flo pulled up to them. She was looking at the horizon.

"Is that what I think it is?" she asked.

A wall of headlights was coming straight towards them.

"Customers?" Sally asked.

"Customers!" Flo cried, her voice edged with

excitement. The town looked great. Maybe this was finally their big chance to get back on the map. "Customers, everybody, and a lot of 'em. You know what to do. Just like we rehearsed."

Suddenly, a helicopter roared overhead, sweeping a light across the town.

"It's the ghost light!" Mater cried. Terrified, he drove away.

"We have found McQueen!" blasted a voice from a PA system. "We have found McQueen!"

The town was suddenly swarming with reporters, photographers and camera vans. The reporters jostled Sally out of the way as they descended on McQueen, asking him questions a mile a minute.

One reporter barked, "Did you have a nervous breakdown, McQueen?"

"Look, McQueen's wearing white-walls!"

"Are your tyres prematurely balding?"

"Stickers?" Sally called. "McQueen?" But her voice was lost in the confusion of the crowd.

"McQueen!" shouted a TV reporter. "Will you still race for the Piston Cup?"

"Sally?" McQueen called. "Sally? Sally!" He searched for the Porsche, but he couldn't find her in the chaos.

Just then, a lorry horn blared. It was Mack! He drove toward McQueen, shoving reporters out of his way.

"You're here!" Mack cried. His voice was thick with tears. "Thank the manufacturers you're alive! Oh, you are a sight for sore headlights. I'm so sorry I lost you, boss. I'll make it up to you."

Mack unhooked the trailer and held back the press so that McQueen could get inside.

"Mack," McQueen said in a dazed voice, "I can't believe you're here."

"Is that the world's fastest racing machine?" boomed a familiar voice.

"Is that Harv?" McQueen asked.

"Yeah, he's in the back," Mack replied.

Then Mack turned to the reporters. "Get back, you oil-thirsty parasites!"

"Harv!" McQueen called into the trailer. "Harv?"

"Kid! I'm over here."

A speakerphone slid easily from the side of the trailer.

"How ya doin', buddy?" McQueen asked into the microphone.

"I'm doing great!" Harv exclaimed. "You're everywhere – radio, TV, the papers. What do you need me for?"

Then the agent's voice turned serious. "That's just a figure of speech. You signed a contract. Where are you? I can't even find you on my GPS."

"I'm in this little town called Radiator Springs," McQueen explained excitedly. "You know Highway 66? It's still here!"

"Yeah, great, kiddo," Harv said, cutting off McQueen. "Playtime is over, pal. While the world's been tryin' to find you, Dinoco's had nobody to woo. Who they gonna woo?"

McQueen knew the answer to that one. "Chick."

"Bingo," Harv said. "Mack, roll the tape."

The TV screen glowed blue, showing footage of Chick standing next to Tex Dinoco. Chick was surrounded by reporters and gorgeous female fans. He even had a new dark thundercloud with a giant *C* painted on him.

"Show us the thunder!" the reporters begged.

"Yeah, give us the thundercloud!"

"You want thunder?" Chick demanded, basking

in the attention. "You want thunder? *Ka-chick-a! Ka-chick-a! Ka-chick-a!*"

"Hey," McQueen said in horror, "that's my bit!"

"You gotta get to Cali pronto," Harv yelled. "Just get out of Radiation Stinks now, or Dinoco is history, you hear me?"

"Yeah, okay," McQueen said slowly, "just give me a second here, Harv." McQueen drove over to Sally, who was parked by the side of the trailer. They looked at each other in silence for a moment.

McQueen spoke first. "Sally, I-I want you to – look, I wish . . . ." He sighed and looked at the ground. He didn't know what to say.

"Thank you," Sally said sincerely. "Thanks for everything."

McQueen looked up at her. "It was just a road."

"No – it was much more than that." Tears welled up in Sally's eyes.

Mack charged over, interrupting them. "We gotta go," he said. "Harv's going crazy. He's gonna have me fired if I don't get you in the truck now."

"Mack, just hold it," McQueen begged. He looked at Sally, pained.

"You should go," Sally told him.

McQueen started to speak, but Sally cut him off. "I hope you find what you're looking for," she told him. Then she backed away and turned, pushing through the press.

"Sally . . ." McQueen called. "Sally!" But it was too late. She had gone.

"C'mon," Harv urged. "Let's go." The agent coaxed McQueen into the trailer. "That's right, kid, let's go. You're a superstar. You don't belong there anyway."

McQueen looked out at the soft neon glow of the town lights one last time before the ramp shut behind him.

As Mack hauled McQueen away, the townsfolk of Radiator Springs watched sadly. Just then, a reporter rolled up to Doc.

"Hey, are you Doc Hudson?" she asked. "Thanks for the call."

Sally's jaw dropped. "You did this?"

"It's best for everyone, Sally," Doc said.

"Best for everyone?" Sally demanded. "Or best for you?"

"Hey, guys!" shouted a reporter. "McQueen's leaving in the truck!"

The press raced after him, leaving the town as suddenly as they had arrived.

"I didn't get to say goodbye to him," Mater said sadly.

One by one, the townsfolk went back to their shops. Alone, Doc sat under the town's traffic light as they all turned off their neon. Radiator Springs was quiet and dark once again.

"Okay, here we go," McQueen said to himself as he sat idling in the darkness of the trailer. It was the day of the Piston-Cup Championship, and McQueen was working hard to find the zone'.

"Focus," he commanded himself. "Speed. I am speed."

Across the country, cars had closed up their shops and headed to the nearest television set to watch the race of the century.

"Bob, there's a crowd of nearly 300,000 cars here at the Los Angeles International Speedway," Darrell said as he and Bob sat in the announcers' booth. "Tickets to this race are hotter than a black leather seat on a hot summer day."

Chick was feeling smug as he basked in the limelight. He was surrounded by press and photographers, soaking up all the attention.

"C'mon, Chick, let's see the cloud!" begged the reporters. "Flash that thunder, baby!"

"Oh, yeah, you wanna know the forecast?" Chick bragged. "I'll give you the forecast: 100 per cent chance of thunder! *Ka-chick-a! Ka-chick-a!* Say it with me!"

Meanwhile, McQueen stayed in his trailer, ignoring the chaos outside. He revved his engine. "Victory," he muttered quietly as he pictured himself flying down the track ahead of Chick and The King. "One winner, two losers. Speed. Speed. Speed!" McQueen remembered the drive with Sally and the view of Radiator Springs from the spot near the Wheel Well. *Gosh, that was gorgeous*, McQueen thought. He smiled a little, picturing the townsfolk. *I never even said goodbye to Mater*, he thought regretfully.

"Hey, Lightning!" Mack called as he banged on the trailer door. "You ready?"

McQueen's eyes snapped open. *What am I doing?* he thought. *I don't have time to daydream – I have a race to win!* "Yeah, yeah, yeah," he said, giving himself a good shake. "I'm ready."

He rolled out of his trailer and faced the enormous crowd of fans. They let out a deafening cheer and McQueen squinted as 1,000 cameras flashed in his face.

"Thanks for being my pit crew today," McQueen said to Mack, who was parked beside a big fuel can.

"Least I could do," Mack replied.

Out on the track, a group of colour-coded cars drove in formation, spelling out the words Piston Cup'.

In the announcers' booth, Bob explained that this would be the last race for Strip Weathers The King.

"You know, Chick Hicks ain't gonna let The King just drive away with it today," Darrell added. "He's gonna pull out all the stops to win this one."

"And there he is," Bob said as the stadium monitor flashed an image of McQueen pulling up to the starting line. "Lightning McQueen. Missing all week and then he turns up in the middle of nowhere, in a little town called Radiator Springs."

"Wearing white-wall tyres," Darrell added with a chuckle, "of all things."

Chick pulled up next to McQueen and flashed his shiny thundercloud. "*Ka-chick-a*! *Ka-chick-a*! *Ka-chick-a*!" He laughed uproariously. "Hey, where ya been, McQueen? I've been kind of lonely, nobody to hang out with – I mean, except the Dinoco folks."

Chick babbled on, but McQueen was having a hard time paying attention to him. His mind was wandering. He was back on the mountain with Sally. *Gee, she looked pretty that day*, McQueen thought as he pictured the beautiful Porsche in front of the waterfall.

Just then, the green flag dropped. Chick and The King were off like bullets.

"*Uuuugh!*" McQueen cried as he snapped out of his daydream. "Shoot!" He took off after them, chasing their bumpers. Two laps later, all three cars were battling for first place.

"Oh, Chick slammed the door on him," Darrell announced as Chick moved in to cut off McQueen. With a sudden burst of speed, Chick left the rookie in his dust.

"Chick's not making it easy on him today," Bob said. It was true. Although he wanted more than ever to win, McQueen was having trouble focusing on the race. His mind kept wandering. Like right then: he was picturing himself on the drive up the mountain with Sally again. He remembered how she had splashed him. And–

A wall!

McQueen jarred himself out of his memory just in time to swerve away from the concrete wall. But he turned too hard and spun deep into the infield. The crowed gasped.

Chick grinned. "Just me and the old man, fellas," he told his pit crew over the radio. "McQueen just doesn't have it today."

20

McQueen idled in the infield, dazed. He could hear The King and Chick speeding around the track – but they seemed far away.

"Kid, you all right?" Mack asked over the radio.

McQueen gave himself a shake, trying to clear his head. He knew that he was losing time. He'd never catch up with the other cars now. "Uh, Mack, I don't know. I don't think–"

Suddenly, a different – and familiar – voice growled over the radio. "I didn't come all this way to see you quit."

McQueen gasped. "Doc?" The rookie peered at pit row, where a crowd was waving at him. Almost everyone was there – Ramone, Flo, Luigi, Guido, Fillmore, Sarge – even Mater. "Guys!" McQueen cried happily. "You're here!"

"Hey, it was Doc's idea, man," Ramone said.

McQueen looked at the crew-chief platform. Doc was there – painted up as the Fabulous Hudson Hornet. He looked glorious. "I knew you needed a crew chief," Doc rumbled, "but I didn't know it was this bad."

"Doc, look at you!" McQueen said in awe. "I thought you said you'd never come back."

"Well, I really didn't have a choice," Doc replied. "Mater didn't get to say goodbye."

"Goodbye!" Mater hollered. He looked at Doc. "Okay, I'm good."

McQueen laughed.

"All right," Doc said, getting down to business, "if you can drive as good as you can fix a road, then you can win this race with your eyes shut. Now, get back out there."

In an instant, McQueen tore onto the track. Suddenly, he felt he had the focus of a laser beam. The team from Radiator Springs let out a cheer as he sped up the asphalt, gaining on Chick and The King.

"We are back in business!" Doc shouted. "Guido,

Luigi – you're going up against professional pit crews, boys. You're gonna have to be fast."

"They will not know what hit them!" Luigi promised.

"Kid, you can beat these guys," Doc said over his headset. "Find the groove that works for you and get those laps back!"

Meanwhile, the monitors showed McQueen's new crew. "Darrell, it appears McQueen has got himself a pit crew," Bob said as the cameras zoomed in on Doc, "and look who he has for a crew chief."

The crowd recognized Doc and began to cheer, welcoming him back.

Bob looked down at pit row in amazement. "Wow, this is history in the making; nobody has seen the racing legend in over 50 years."

But history was happening on the track, too, as McQueen whipped past Chick and The King.

"McQueen's coming up fast! He goes three wide and passes them on the inside!" Bob announced excitedly. He couldn't believe it.

"What?" Chick was shocked as McQueen slid

past, making up the first of his two lost laps.

Back in Radiator Springs, Sally, Lizzie and Red watched McQueen on television.

"C'mon! You got it, Stickers!" Sally exclaimed.

Making up his second lap, McQueen closed in on Chick and The King again.

"Oh," Chick muttered, "kid's just trying to be a hero, huh?" With a sudden jerk, Chick knocked McQueen as he started to pass. "Well, what do you think of this?" He sneered as McQueen spun around until he was facing backwards.

But McQueen didn't slow down. He bolted past Chick – in reverse.

"Whoa!" Mater whooped from pit row. "I taught him that. *Ka-chow*!"

"What a move by McQueen!" Bob cried as he looked down on the race from the booth. "He's caught up to the leaders!"

"A three-way battle for the lead with ten to go," Darrell continued.

21

McQueen was giving the race everything he had. He was hard on Chick's tail, but Chick was doing everything in his power to block McQueen. There was the grind of scraping metal as the two cars rubbed together. "No, you don't–" Chick snarled.

Just then, one of McQueen's tyres burst. "Doc, I'm flat," he cried. "I'm flat!"

"Bring it in," Doc commanded as the yellow flag dropped, signalling that there was debris on the track. That meant the race was temporarily suspended; the other cars had to slow down and follow the pace car while the debris was removed. "Don't tear yourself up, kid."

Doc knew that they had to get McQueen back onto the track before the pace car came around. Otherwise, McQueen would fall behind again.

"Guido!" Doc shouted. "It's time."

"Hey, tiny," one of Chick's pitties teased, "you gonna clean his windshield?"

Chick's pitties laughed as McQueen pulled in. But Guido ignored them. This was his lifelong dream – to give the ultimate pit stop. And he was ready.

In one fluid movement, Guido tossed the tyres into the air and bolted them onto McQueen before they could hit the ground.

Guido looked at Chick's stunned pit crew and blew on his torque gun. Then he offered the only English he knew. "Pit stop."

"Guido, you did it!" Luigi cried as McQueen pulled back onto the track, moving into place behind the pace car.

"Did you see that, Bob?" Darrell cried from the announcers' booth.

Bob gaped in awe. "That was the fastest pit stop I've ever seen!"

On the track, the green flag dropped and the three cars surged forward, racing at a furious pace.

"This is it!" Bob announced with excitement. "We're heading into the final lap and McQueen is right behind the leaders. What a comeback!"

"This is it, kiddo," Doc said as McQueen closed in on Chick and The King. "You got four turns left. One at a time. Drive it in deep and hope it sticks."

McQueen headed towards the first turn, eyes narrowing with determination.

"Go!" Doc cried, and McQueen did.

He pushed everything he had into high gear. Seeing his rival make his move, Chick cut quickly to bash McQueen against a wall. But McQueen was too fast; Chick missed him.

But Chick didn't slow down. Instead, he drove forwards, ramming his front bumper into McQueen's rear. McQueen spun wildly towards the infield.

But McQueen wasn't about to give up. At the last moment, he cut right to go left, just the way Doc had taught him. With a smooth swerve, he shot back onto the track – in the lead!

"McQueen has taken the lead!" Darrell announced to the audience. "Lightning McQueen is going to win the Piston Cup!"

Chick and The King had fallen behind

McQueen. But Chick wasn't giving up, either. If he couldn't win, he could at least come in second. "I'm not coming in behind you again, old man!" he cried as he rammed The King, causing The King to spin into the wall.

Crash!

The crowd gasped as The King stopped in the infield, battered, dented and unable to move.

McQueen was moving towards the finish line when he heard the boos. Confused, he looked at the giant television screen and saw The King. He wasn't moving.

An image of Doc flashed into McQueen's mind: Doc had looked the same way in the photo of the Fabulous Hudson Hornet's famous crash.

McQueen screeched to a stop right before the finish line.

"Yeah!" Chick hollered as he shot past McQueen. "Woo-hoo! I won, baby! Yeah! Oh, yeah! Woo-hoo-hoo!"

"What's he doing, Doc?" Flo whispered as she watched McQueen. He was inches from the finish line and still hadn't moved.

Suddenly, McQueen put himself into reverse and headed back to The King.

"What are you doing, kid?" The King asked as McQueen approached. He was completely wiped out, but not completely broken; McQueen could see that.

"I think The King should finish his last race," McQueen said humbly. And then, as gently as he could, McQueen began to push The King towards the finish line.

"You just gave up the Piston Cup," The King pointed out, "you know that?"

"Ah, this grumpy old race car I know once told me something," McQueen said as he helped The King to the end of the track. "It's just an empty cup." Doc smiled proudly as he listened on his radio.

Meanwhile, Chick was hooting in triumph, circling in the infield. "Woo-hoo-hoo!" It took him a moment to realize that no one was cheering with him. In fact, no one was even watching him. "Hey, what?" He stopped in his tracks. "What's going on?"

McQueen pushed The King across the finish line and the crowd erupted in cheers! The stadium went crazy at the sight of one of the proudest moments in racing history.

"Way to go, buddy!" Mater hollered.

Tears welled up in Fillmore's eyes. "There's a lot of love out there, you know, man?"

"Don't embarrass me, Fillmore," Sarge grunted.

The only one who wasn't impressed was Chick. He raced onto the winner's platform impatiently. "Come on, baby," he said. "Bring it out, bring out the Piston Cup. *Ka-chick-a*! *Ka-chick-a*!"

But nobody came out to deliver the cup. Instead, someone tossed it onto the stage, where it clattered to the floor beside Chick. No one cheered.

"Now, that's what I'm talking about right there, yeah!" Chick crowed. He looked around at the silent spectators. "Hey, how come the only one celebrating is me, huh? Where are the girls? Come on, where's the fireworks? Bring on the confetti!"

A confetti cannon let out a shot and hit Chick's bumper hard. "*Owww*! Hey, easy with the confetti. What's going on? Come on, snap some cameras, let's wrap this up. I gotta go sign my deal with

Dinoco," Chick said, starting to realize that no one cared.

The crowd started to boo.

"What's wrong with everybody?" Chick demanded as a few of the cars started throwing rubbish onto the stage. "Hey! Hey! This is the start of the Chick era!" Chick finally gave up, grabbed his Piston Cup and rolled away.

But McQueen didn't pay attention to any of that. He was too busy pushing The King towards the Dinoco tent. Then, as The King's wife hurried over to give her husband a kiss, McQueen quietly headed to the Rust-eze tent. His whole pit crew had gathered there – along with the goofy brothers from Rust-eze, who had given McQueen his start in racing.

"You made us proud, kid," one of the brothers said affectionately.

"Congrats on the loss, me bucko," Mack said.

Doc smiled at the younger racing car. "You got a lotta stuff, kid."

"Thanks, Doc."

"Hey, Lightning!" Tex Dinoco called from the

front of the Dinoco tent. "How about comin' over here and talking to me a minute?"

McQueen drove over to join him.

"Son, that was some real racin' out there," Tex said to McQueen. "How'd you like to become the new face of Dinoco?"

McQueen looked up at the fancy Dinoco tent area. The helicopter gave him a wink.

"But I didn't win," McQueen pointed out.

"Lightnin'," Tex went on, "there's a whole lot more to racin' than just winnin'."

McQueen was tempted. It was everything he had always dreamed of. Dinoco was a great company with a lot of money. And Tex seemed like a really great guy. Still . . . .

McQueen looked at the Rust-eze tent, where the two brothers were telling their usual lousy jokes. He couldn't help smiling.

"Thank you, Mr Tex," McQueen told the mogul, "but those Rust-eze guys over there gave me my big break. I think I'm gonna stick with them."

"Well, I sure can respect that," Tex said sincerely. "Still, you know, if there's ever anything

I can do for you, just let me know."

"I sure appreciate that. Thank you." McQueen thought for a moment. "Actually," he said, "there is *one* thing."

22

"*Woo-hoo!*" Mater hollered, leaning out of the window of the Dinoco helicopter as it flew over the Wheel Well. "Hey, hey! Hey, look at me! I'm flyin'!"

It was two days later, and Radiator Springs was hopping. A glistening red Ferrari and two black Maseratis had just rolled into Luigi's tyre shop.

"So," the Ferrari said to Luigi, "Lightning McQueen told me this was the best place in the world to get tyres. How about setting me and my friends up with three or four sets each?"

Luigi gasped. It was Michael Schumacher! "Guido . . ." he cried. "There is a real Michael Schumacher Ferrari in-a my store! A real Ferrari! Punch me, Guido! Punch me in the face. This is the most glorious day of my life!"

Luigi fainted in their presence.

The Ferrari turned to Guido. "I hope your little friend's okay," he said in Italian. "I hear wonderful things about your store."

Guido gaped at the Ferrari. Then he fainted, too.

Sally was at the Wheel Well, looking down on the town, when McQueen appeared beside her. He was decked out in his full Radiator-Springs paint and stickers.

"*Ka-chow!*" he said.

They both laughed.

"Just passin' through?" Sally asked.

"Actually," McQueen said, keeping his voice casual, "I thought I'd stop and stay a while." He leaned towards Sally. "I hear this place is back on the map," he said in a confidential whisper.

Sally gave him a dubious look. "It is?"

"Yeah, there's a rumour floating around that some hotshot Piston-Cup race car is setting up his big racing headquarters here," McQueen replied.

Sally's eyes widened. "Really?" she asked, then caught herself. "Oh, well," she said, playing it cool. "There goes the town."

"You know," McQueen whispered, "I really missed you, Sally." The racing car leaned closer to her.

"McQueen and Sally, parked beneath a tree!" Mater shouted as the helicopter flew past.

"K-I-S-S . . . uh . . . I-N-T!"

"Great timing, Mater!" McQueen shouted. He looked at Sally. "He's my best friend," he explained with a shrug. "What are you gonna do?"

"So, Stickers," Sally said, giving him a playful grin. "Last one to Flo's buys?"

"I don't know, why don't we just take a drive?" McQueen suggested.

Sally's eyes twinkled. "Naah." Then she suddenly sped off down the mountain.

"Yeah!" McQueen shouted as he zoomed after her. "*Ka-chow!*"

Disney PRESENTS A PIXAR FILM

Cars

DISNEY · PIXAR
TOY STORY 2

Book of the Film

First published by Parragon in 2007
Parragon
Queen Street House
4 Queen Street
Bath BA1 1HE, UK

Copyright © 2007 Disney Enterprises, Inc. / Pixar
Mr. Potato Head® and Mrs. Potato Head® are registered
trademarks of Hasbro, Inc. Used with permission. © Hasbro, Inc.
Slinky® Dog © James Industries.
Etch A Sketch® © The Ohio Art Company.
Troll Doll © Russ Berrie and Company, Inc.

All rights reserved. No part of this publication may be reproduced,
stored in a retrieval system or transmitted, in any form or by any
means, electronic, mechanical, photocopying, recording or
otherwise, without the prior permission of the copyright holder.

ISBN 978-1-4075-1810-7

Printed in China

DISNEY · PIXAR
TOY STORY 2

Book of the Film

Adapted by Leslie Goldman

PaRragon

Chapter One

Buzz Lightyear sped through the dark sky, his blinking spacesuit lights flashing. He zeroed in on his target – a huge red planet. As the clouds surrounding the planet drifted away, he soared through, landing smoothly on the rocky surface. He raised his wrist communicator to contact his headquarters.

"Buzz Lightyear mission log: all signs point to this planet as the location of Zurg's fortress." Buzz glanced up and down the surface of the deserted planet. "But there seems to be no sign of intelligent life anywhere."

Just as he was starting to relax, Buzz spotted a group of red laser beams. Seconds later, he was surrounded by armed robot forces. He raised his laser gun towards a crystal formation nearby and fired. A huge explosion blew the robots away. But he hadn't destroyed the enemy completely. From the wall of the crater, a robotic camera moved swiftly towards Buzz. He took aim once more and fired.

He was able to destroy the camera, but then he felt something shifting under his feet. Before he could move, the ground gave way beneath him and he fell into a long, dark, deep cavern. Buzz landed on the ground and spotted a maze. There was no other way to go, so he entered.

A blinking orange dot was on his back, though. The evil Zurg was monitoring Buzz's every step.

"Come to me, my prey," Zurg growled from his control room.

Buzz walked through a door and it closed behind him. Suddenly, deadly spikes shot out of the door and zoomed towards Buzz. He ran down the tunnel and jumped through another door without a millisecond to spare. The spikes banged against the closed door, piercing the exterior. Buzz was safe for now. He walked over a thin, swinging rope bridge with stealth, only to come face to face with Zurg.

"Buzz Lightyear! Your defeat will be my greatest triumph!" yelled Zurg, as he took aim with his ion blaster.

"Not today, Zurg," bellowed Buzz.

He raised his shield, deflecting Zurg's bullet. Then he hurled the shield at Zurg, hitting him directly in the face.

Momentarily stunning Zurg, Buzz leaped over him, and fired one shot. It went to Zurg's left, narrowly missing its target.

Zurg recovered and took aim again, blasting Buzz and blowing his torso off.

"Ahh-ha-ha!" laughed a triumphant Zurg.

GAME OVER flashed in red across the screen.

Chapter Two

Andy Davis was out of sight, so his toys were playing on their own. The real Buzz Lightyear and his friend and fellow toy Rex, a plastic dinosaur, jumped up to the screen.

"Ooooh, now that's gotta hurt," Buzz said in sympathy.

Rex stomped his feet. "No! I'm never gonna defeat Zurg! I give up," he shouted.

"Come on. Pull yourself together, Rex. Remember, a Space Ranger must turn and face his fears no matter how ugly it gets. You must not flinch!"

"Okay, one more round," Rex said,

ready to give it another try. He turned back to the TV screen. "Aaah!" yelled Rex. Woody's sudden reflection across the video screen scared him.

Ignoring Rex's whimpering, Woody looked down at his magic erase clipboard and spoke to Buzz.

"Okay, here's a list of things to do while I'm gone. Batteries need to be changed. Toys in the bottom of the chest need to be rotated. And make sure everyone attends Mr Spell's seminar on 'what to do if you or a part of you is swallowed'. Okay?"

Buzz shook his head. "Woody, you haven't found your hat yet, have you?"

"No," said Woody. "Andy's leaving for cowboy camp any minute now, and I can't find it anywhere!"

"Don't worry. In just a few hours you'll be sitting around a crackling campfire with Andy making delicious hot schmoes," said Buzz.

"They're called s'mores, Buzz."

"Right," nodded Buzz. "Has anyone found

Woody's hat yet?" he called to the rest of the toys.

Green Army Men swarmed around the open toy box. Some abseiled down from the open lid into the box. "Hut. Hut. Hut . . ." they chanted.

The sergeant approached Buzz and saluted. "Negatory. Still searching."

Hamm, the piggy bank, sat on the windowsill, looking outside through Lenny, the toy binoculars.

"The lawn gnome next door says it's not in the yard, but he'll keep looking," Hamm reported back.

Bo Peep and the Troll Doll walked into the room.

"It's not in Molly's room. We've looked everywhere," shrugged Bo Peep.

Mr Potato Head peeked out from under the bed.

"I found it," he shouted.

"You found my hat?" cheered Woody.

"Your hat? Nah. The missus lost her earring again. Oh, my little sweet potato?"

He held up a plastic ear with a dangling earring attached.

Mrs Potato Head walked up with a huge grin painted on her face.

"You found it! It's so good to have a big strong spud around the house!"

She took the ear and plugged it back into her ear socket.

Woody walked over to Andy's packed duffel bags and kicked one of them.

"Great. That's just great! This'll be the first year I miss cowboy camp, all because of my stupid hat."

"Woody, look under your boot," said Bo.

"Bo, don't be silly. My hat's not under my boot."

"Just look," she said.

Woody sighed, and then raised his foot and looked at it.

"There, see? No hat. Just the word *Andy*."

"Uh-huh," said Bo, smiling. "And the boy who wrote that would take you to camp with or without your hat."

Woody stared at the signature and smiled. Bo was right.

"I'm sorry, Bo. It's just that I've been looking forward to this all year. It's my one time with just me and Andy."

Bo grinned, and snared Woody with the crook of her stick. She pulled him towards her.

"You're cute when you care."

"Everyone's looking," whispered a blushing Woody.

"Let 'em look," she said, and kissed him.

Someone turned on the TV. A chicken clucking blared from the set. It was an advert. A large man dressed in a chicken suit was flapping his wings atop Al's Toy Barn.

"Hey, kids," he clucked. "This is Al, from Al's Toy Barn. And I'm sitting on some good deals here . . . Ow! Ah think I'm feelin' a deal hatchin' right now! Let's see what we got!"

The man squinted and squirmed, and then stood up to reveal a giant egg. It cracked open and a giant dollar bill appeared. A crowd of toys floated across the screen.

"We got boats for a buck, beanies for a buck, boomerangs . . ."

"Turn it off," shouted Woody. "Someone's going to hear."

The TV blared, "Banjos for a buck, buck, buck!" Al flapped his chicken wings. "And that's cheap, cheap, cheap!"

A map flashed on the screen, and Al pointed to the Toy Barn.

Hamm waddled forward, grabbed the remote and turned off the TV.

"I despise that chicken," he complained.

Slinky inched his wiry silver body into the room.

"Okay," he gasped, out of breath. "I got good news and I got bad news."

"What, what?" asked the toys.

"Good news is, I found Woody's hat!"

Slinky wagged his tail – upon which

Woody's hat was perched.

"My hat!" shouted Woody. "Aw, Slink . . . thank you! Thank you!"

"What's the bad news?" asked Buzz.

"Here it comes!" shouted Slinky.

Chapter Three

A sniffing sound pierced through the low chatter. It got louder, and then even louder, and then it turned into a bark.

"Aaah!" shouted Rex. "It's Buster!"

The toys all rushed to the door in an attempt to block out the inevitable. Rocky strained, but the pressure was too great. The dog's wet nose nudged through the crack in the door. And the toys knew it wasn't stopping there.

"Woody! Hide! Quick!" called Bo.

With a yelp, Woody dived into Andy's duffel bag and burrowed underneath some clothes and a baseball mitt.

Suddenly the door creaked open.

Buster, a caramel-coloured dachshund, jumped triumphantly to the centre of the room. He barked loudly and ran around the room, scattering toys and drool everywhere.

Etch spun quickly, in order to avoid Buster. But Buster, noticing the movement, pounced, flattening him. Buster panted and looked around. Drool dripped from his mouth and he continued his rampage.

As soon as Buster moved on, Etch wobbled to a standing position. The remains of his picture were covered with paw prints.

Suddenly Buster sniffed and turned towards the pile of bags. He ran over to the duffel, pulled Woody out and flung him. Woody landed in the centre of the room, lifeless.

Buster jumped on top of Woody, lips curled. He growled for a second, and then began to lick him.

"Okay, okay," spluttered Woody. "You found me, Buster. All right. Hey, how'd he do that, Hamm?"

Hamm stood in front of Mr Spell's readout of 13.5 seconds.

"Eh, looks like a new record!"

Woody snapped his fingers. "Okay, boy. Sit. Stick 'em up! Pow!"

With a happy yelp, Buster fell over and played dead.

"Great job, boy," said Woody, scratching Buster's belly. "Who's gonna miss me while I'm gone? Who's gonna miss me?"

Suddenly, voices from the hallway drifted into Andy's bedroom.

"Andy? Have you got all your stuff?" asked Andy's mum, Mrs Davis.

"It's in my room," said Andy.

Woody gasped and ran off to take his position. All of the other toys froze where they were and lay lifeless.

Andy kicked his bedroom door open wide with one cowboy boot. He walked in, revealing his full cowboy outfit. Buster barked and ran to Andy.

"Stick 'em up," shouted Andy, pulling his toy guns out of their holster on his belt.

Buster left the room, and headed down the stairs.

"I guess we'll work on that later," Andy said, putting down his toy guns.

He walked up to Woody, who was propped up on his bag.

"Hey, Woody. Ready to go to cowboy camp?"

"Andy, honey," called his mother. "Five minutes and we're leaving."

Andy began to play with Woody. He picked up Buzz, too. They began to shake hands, but to Andy's shock and dismay, Woody's arm ripped!

"Andy, let's go," called Mrs Davis. She poked her head into Andy's room. "What's wrong?" she asked.

"Woody's arm ripped!" gasped Andy.

"Maybe we can fix him on the way?" Mrs Davis suggested.

"No, let's just leave him," sighed Andy, tossing Woody aside.

"I'm sorry, honey. But you know, toys don't last forever."

Mrs Davis placed Woody on the highest shelf in Andy's room, amidst a pile of old books. Then she and Andy left the room.

Seconds later, the toys came back to life. They stared up at Woody.

"What just happened?" they questioned.

"Woody's been shelved," cried Mr Potato Head.

Woody scrambled to the edge of his shelf and looked out of the window. Andy and his mother were getting into their van. Sadly he watched as the van pulled away.

Chapter Four

It was a long, hot summer on the shelf. The sun rose early one August morning. Woody was shaken from his sleep by the sound of a van pulling up in front of the house. Once more, he looked out of the window.

Andy jumped out of the car, riding a hobby horse.

"Yee-haw! Ride 'em, cowboy! Whoa! Yeah! Giddyap! Giddyap!"

"He's back," Woody whispered.

He glanced down. Rex, Slinky, Mr Potato Head and Rocky were sitting and playing cards at the foot of the bed.

"Hey, everybody! Andy's back! He's back early from cowboy camp!"

They heard Andy bound up the steps.

"Places everyone! Andy's coming," yelled Hamm.

The toys dropped their cards and scattered. Woody froze in his 'toy pose' just as Andy burst into the room. Andy ran up to Woody and pulled him down from the shelf.

"Hey, Woody! Did you miss me? Giddyap, giddyap. Ride 'em, cowboy!"

Andy walked Woody across the floor and swung his arms. Suddenly, Andy's smile faded.

"Oh, I forgot," he said to Woody. "You're broken." He stared at Woody, frowning. "I don't want to play with you any more."

And with that, Andy dropped Woody.

Woody landed, forlorn, in a rubbish bin filled with broken toy parts. Struggling, he tried to crawl out of the bin.

"Andy!" he yelled, struggling as toy arms pulled him back to the bottom of the bin.

Andy stared into the bin.

"Bye, Woody!" He closed the lid.

Woody woke up with a start. He was still on Andy's shelf.

"Huh? What's going on?"

He glanced around the room, confused. Then he realized that it had all been a bad dream. He got up and his broken arm bumped into a pile of books, knocking them over. A pile of dust rose, and Woody coughed. Soon he noticed that he wasn't the only one coughing.

"What's going on? Wheezy, is that you?" he said to a small stuffed penguin.

"Hey, Woody," gasped Wheezy.

"What are you doing up here?" said Woody, confused. "I thought Mum took you to get your squeaker fixed months ago. Andy was so upset . . ."

"Nah," said Wheezy, motioning with one fuzzy wing. "She just told Andy that to calm him down. Then she shelved me."

"Why didn't you yell for help?" asked Woody.

"I tried squeaking," shrugged Wheezy. "But I'm still broken. No one could hear me."

Wheezy squinted his eyes and tried to squeak. The only sound that emerged was a pathetic, wavery little yelp.

He coughed again and explained, "The dust aggravates my condition. Cough, hack, wheeze!"

Wheezy fell into Woody's arms, exhausted.

"What's the point of prolonging the inevitable?" Wheezy gasped. "We're all just one stitch away from here . . . to there." He pointed outside.

Woody looked out of the window and gasped. Mrs Davis was pounding a YARD SALE sign into the ground.

Chapter Five

Woody called down to the other toys.

"Yard sale! Yard sale! Wake up, everyone! There's a yard sale outside!"

Buzz and Slinky stirred from their snooze.

"Huh?" asked Slinky, stretching out his coiled body.

"Yard sale?" questioned Buzz.

Sharky, Snake and Troll all popped their heads out of Andy's toy chest.

"Sarge! Emergency roll call," said Woody.

Sarge burst out from the Bucket-O-Soldiers, saluting Woody.

"Sir! Yes, sir!" He went around to gather all of the toys. "Red alert!" he called through his mini microphone. "All civilians fall into position! NOW!"

The toys responded quickly and lined up.

"Single file! Let's move, move, move!"

Buzz marched over and began to write on the magic slate.

"Hamm?" he called.

"Here," Hamm shouted.

"Potato Head, Mr and Mrs?"

"Here," said Mrs Potato Head.

Buzz continued the roll call. "Slinky?"

"Yo."

Rex quivered. "Oh, I hate yard sales."

Suddenly there was a bump from behind Andy's door.

"Ahh, someone's coming!" Rex warned everyone.

The toys resumed their old positions and froze. Woody hid Wheezy back behind the ABC book on the shelf. Woody returned to his old place as soon as the door began to creak open.

Mrs Davis entered with a box marked 25 CENTS. She dug under Andy's bed and placed a pair of blue-and-silver Velcro shoes in the box. She picked up Rex, who tried to hide his look of utter panic. Luckily, she placed Rex on a table. She was merely moving him to get to the puzzle that he was sitting on. Next she reached up to the top shelf where Woody and Wheezy were, and took the ABC book. Woody sighed, but seconds later, Mrs Davis reached for Wheezy.

"HSSSS . . . HSSSS" squeaked Wheezy, as he was dropped into the box. "Bye, Woody," he whispered, as he was carried out of the room.

Woody gasped. "Not Wheezy. Oh, c'mon, think, Woody, think . . . think."

He had to do something. Woody raised his good arm and let out a loud whistle. Buster came bounding into the room.

"Here, boy. Here, Buster, up here!" called Woody.

He tried to climb down, but slipped because of his bad arm. He began to fall towards the hardwood floor. Buster scrambled towards Woody and was able to catch him at the last second.

"Ooof!" groaned Woody. He propped himself up on Buster's back, and patted his matted fur. "Okay, boy, to the yard sale."

"Did he say yard sale?" Mr Potato Head asked the others.

"He's crazy!" agreed the toys.

Chapter Six

Out on the front lawn, Woody and Buster hid behind an armchair at the edge of the yard sale. They peered around the chair, checking to see if the coast was clear.

"Okay, boy," Woody whispered into Buster's ear. "Let's go, boy. And keep it casual."

They inched their way over towards the table with the 25 CENTS box. Buster paused at the edge of the table, and Woody jumped on. He hid for a moment behind a tall pepper grinder. Then he ran over to the box, hoisted himself up and jumped inside.

Seconds later, Woody was able to recover Wheezy. He pushed Wheezy up and over the edge of the box, and then jumped out himself. They both ran to Buster. Woody tucked Wheezy into Buster's collar.

"There you go, pal."

"Bless you, Woody," wheezed Wheezy.

"All right now, back to Andy's room, where we belong," Woody said, as he climbed onto Buster's back himself.

"Way to go, cowboy!" yelled the other toys, who were watching from the window.

They bounced back to victory, but then Wheezy started to slip out from under Buster's collar.

"Woody . . . I'm slip'n . . . oh, oh," he chanted with each bounce.

Woody held on to Wheezy with his good arm. But when Buster had to jump over a skateboard in their path, Woody was thrown to the ground. The oblivious hound kept on running, leaving Woody flat on his back in the grass.

Woody lifted his head and watched Buster and Wheezy make their way back into the house. He groaned, but indeed, the worst was yet to come.

"Mummy, mummy! Look at this!" yelled a little girl. Her body cast a large shadow over Woody. "It's a cowboy dolly . . ."

Back in Andy's room, the toys watched the scene in horror. Buzz looked through the binoculars. "No, no, no . . ."

"That's not her toy!" shouted Rex.

"What does that little gal think she's doing?" asked Slinky.

The girl picked up Woody and ran to her mother. "Mummy, can we keep him? Please?"

"Oh, honey, we're not going to buy any broken toys," her mother said, staring at Woody's limp arm. She took Woody from her daughter and placed him on a nearby table.

Mrs Davis didn't notice, but someone else did. A big man with a goatee gasped and ran over to Woody. "Original hand-painted face, natural dyed blanket-stitched vest . . ." He picked up Woody and grinned. "Hmmm, a little rip . . . fixable. Oh, if only you had your hand-stitched polyvinyl–"

The man suddenly spotted Woody's hat on the ground.

"Hat!" he yelped. "Oh, I found him! I found him! I found him!"

Mrs Davis walked over to the man.

"Excuse me. Can I help you?" she asked.

He looked up. "Oh, ah, I'll give you, ah, fifty cents for all this junk."

"Oh, now, how did this get here?" said Mrs Davis, reaching for Woody.

"Oh, a pro," laughed the man. "Very well . . . five dollars."

"I'm sorry." Mrs Davis shook her head. "It's an old family toy."

She took Woody from the man and

began to walk away.

He got out his wallet and followed Mrs Davis.

"Wait, wait! I'll give you fifty bucks for him!" he said, waving the cash in front of Mrs Davis.

"He's not for sale," she answered.

"Everything's for sale," reasoned the man. "Or, or trade . . . ummm, you like my watch?"

"Sorry," said Mrs Davis, shaking her head. She put Woody in the cash box and locked it.

The man lurked around the yard sale, waiting for the perfect moment when Mrs Davis would be distracted. When she turned her back, he pried open the cash box and grabbed Woody.

Hiding Woody in his suitcase, he ran to his car. He dropped the bag into the back seat through the open window, got quickly into the car and took off . . . tyres screeching as he tore down the street.

Woody bounced around inside the

suitcase. Shaken and terrified, he wondered how he was going to get back to Andy. Woody heard the car stop and the door open, and then he was lifted out. He unzipped the bag and peered out. He noticed a sign and shuddered.

The sign read NO CHILDREN ALLOWED.

Chapter Seven

Back in Andy's room, the toys gathered around to plan a way to get Woody back. Hamm stood in front of Etch, pacing.

"All right," he said. "Let's review this one more time." He tapped his pointer on the Etch A Sketch, where Woody's figure was drawn. "At precisely 8:32-ish, Exhibit A, Woody, was kidnapped. The composite sketch of the kidnapper . . ."

Etch quickly erased Woody, and then drew a short fat guy with a beard that almost touched his feet, it was so long.

"He didn't have a beard like that," protested Bo.

"Fine," said Hamm. "Etch, give him a shave."

Etch erased the man and drew another one, without the beard.

"The kidnapper was bigger than that," said Slinky.

"I know he wore glasses," said Bo.

"Yeah, he's too small," the other toys agreed.

"Oh, picky, picky, picky," complained Hamm.

"Just go straight to Exhibit F!" said an impatient Mr Potato Head.

Exhibit F was a street and traffic scene constructed out of Lincoln Logs. Pointing to a matchbox car, Mr Potato Head traced the route of the car.

"The kidnapper's vehicle fled the scene in this direction."

"Your eyes are on backwards," said Hamm. "It went the other way."

"Excuse me. A little quiet please," said Buzz.

He was studying Mr Spell, whose

screen was lit up with the word LZTYBRN.

The toys approached Buzz.

"What are you doing?" asked Rex.

"I managed to catch the licence plate of the car Woody was taken in," Buzz explained. "There's some sort of message encoded on that vehicle's ID tag."

Mr Spell gave some suggestions.

"Lazy, Toy, Brain. Lousy, Try, Brian. Liz, Try, Bran."

"It's just a licence plate . . . it's just a jumble of letters," said Mr Potato Head.

"Yeah, and there are about 3.5 million registered cars in the tricounty area alone," said Hamm, turning back to the Etch A Sketch.

"Lazy, Try, Brian," Mr Spell continued.

"Oh, this can't help. Let's just leave Buzz to play with his toys," said Mr Potato Head.

The other toys started to retreat, when Buzz cracked the code.

"Toy, toy, toy!" he yelled.

"Al's Toy Barn," said Mr Spell.

"Al's Toy Barn!" they all repeated.

Buzz spun around and ran to Etch.

"Draw that man in the chicken suit!" he said.

When Etch had finished the drawing, the toys stared in amazement.

"It's the chicken man!" gasped Rex.

"That's our guy," said Buzz.

"I knew there was something I didn't like about that chicken!" said Hamm.

Chapter Eight

Al stomped into his apartment in full chicken suit gear. He grabbed his mobile phone and started yelling into it.

"Yeah, yeah, yeah. I'll be right there. And we're gonna do this commercial in one take, do you hear me? Because I am in the middle of something really important!"

He hung up and stared at Woody, who was now trapped behind a glass case.

"You, my little cowboy friend, are going to make me big . . ." he began to flap his wings, ". . . buck, buck, bucks," he finished, laughing.

When Al left the room, Woody rammed his shoulder into the door of the glass case. After a few pushes, he was able to open it. He jumped to the floor and rushed over to the door. The handle was way out of reach, and he couldn't open it. Instead, he jumped up to a chair and onto the windowsill.

Woody gasped when he got a glimpse outside. There were tall buildings everywhere, and it was clear that he was far from home.

"Andy," he sighed, wistfully.

Woody jumped down from the windowsill and began to explore Al's apartment. Suddenly, a floppy toy horse slipped through his legs.

"Whoa-oa-oa!" yelled Woody, as the horse leaped around like a bucking bronco. Woody struggled to hang on. "Hey, stop! Horsey, stop! Sit, boy! Whoa! Sit, I say!"

The horse sat down, causing Woody to tumble to the floor. His legs flipped over his head. He was upside down when he noticed a cowgirl doll standing in front of him.

"Yee-haw!" she yelled, and grabbed Woody, straightening him up. "It's you! It's you!" She rubbed her knuckles on his head. "It's really you!"

"What's me?" asked Woody, backing away.

"Whoo-wee!" exclaimed the cowgirl.

She spun Woody around like a swing dancer, and held on to his pull string. She yanked him back and caught him with her other arm. Then she put her ear to his chest to listen. "There's a snake in my boot!" said Woody's voice box.

"Ha!" said the cowgirl, slapping Woody on the back. "It is you!"

"Please stop saying that," pleaded Woody. "What is going on here?"

"Say hello to Prospector," said the cowgirl.

She whistled to the horse, who dived into the cardboard box, dug around and pulled out an old miner doll, wrapped in his own original plastic casing.

"You remember the Prospector, don't you?" she asked.

"Oh, we've waited countless years for this day! It's so good to see you, Woody," said the Prospector, who was dressed in mining clothes and had a plastic pick hanging from his belt.

"Listen, I don't know what . . . hey! How did you know my name?" asked Woody.

"Everyone knows your name, Woody," said the cowgirl.

"You mean, you don't know who we are?" asked the Prospector. "Bullseye?"

Bullseye the horse galloped up onto the boxes and turned on the lights. Woody glanced around the room and gasped. He was surrounded by the complete set: 'Woody's Roundup Collection'.

There were boxes and boxes of toys: a tractor, the horse and an entire ranch. There was a Woody yo-yo, a cereal box and even a magazine cover with a close-up of

Woody's face.

Prospector nodded at Bullseye, and the horse pushed a videotape into the VCR. Jessie turned on the TV with the remote. A pair of barn doors flashed up on the screen. The title card read COWBOY CRUNCHIES PRESENTS.

The TV announcer boomed, "Cowboy Crunchies, the only cereal that's sugar-frosted and dipped in chocolate, proudly presents . . . *Woody's Roundup*! Starring Jessie, the yodelling cowgirl!"

A doll just like the cowgirl danced on to the screen.

"Yo-de-lay-he-hoo!" she bellowed.

A mass of animals fell from the sky – skunks, rabbits, armadillos, a squirrel – surrounding Jessie. They squealed and squeaked.

"Look! That's me," shouted Jessie. She jumped up and down and pointed at the screen enthusiastically.

Woody stared from the screen to Jessie, and then back to the screen again. He felt utterly confused.

The TV announcer continued, "The sharpest horse in the West . . ." as Bullseye galloped on to the screen.

"Stinky Pete, the Prospector!"

On screen, the Prospector emerged from a cardboard mine.

"Has anyone seen my pick?" he asked.

The Prospector smiled at Woody.

"The best is yet to come," he whispered, nodding at the screen.

"And the high-ridin'est, rootin' tootin'est hero of all time – Sheriff Woody!"

Woody watched as his onscreen self burst forward, leaped onto Bullseye and reared up.

"Hey howdy hey, Sheriff Woody," shouted the audience of kids. Dozens of them were wearing cowboy hats, waving and cheering at their hero.

As the facts came together for Woody, his shock turned to joy. He had once been a big star!

Chapter Nine

Back at Andy's house, the toys gathered around the TV. They went from channel to channel, searching for the Al's Toy Barn commercial. When they found it, Etch quickly sketched a copy of the map, placing a bold 'X' on the spot that marked the Toy Barn.

"That's where I need to go!" announced Buzz, pointing at the X.

"You can't go alone," said Rex. "You'll never make it there."

"Woody once risked his life to save me. I couldn't call myself his friend if I weren't willing to do the same," explained Buzz. "So who's with me?"

He glanced around the room, waiting for volunteers.

Mrs Potato Head filled Mr Potato Head's rear compartment with attachments.

"I'm packing you an extra pair of shoes, and your *angry* eyes, just in case," she said to him.

Bo grabbed Buzz and kissed him on the cheek. "This is for Woody – when you find him," she said.

Buzz blushed.

"All right, but I don't think it'll mean the same . . . coming from me," he said.

Slinky, Mr Potato Head, Rex, Buzz and Hamm walked across the rooftop towards the edge. Mr Potato Head grabbed the end of Slinky's coil and jumped off the roof, using Slinky as a bungee cord.

"Geronimo!" he yelled, as he landed safely on the lawn below.

Hamm jumped next, and then Rex. Buzz walked back to the window.

"We'll be back before Andy gets home,"

he told the others.

The toys inside gathered at the window and waved goodbye.

"To Al's Toy Barn – and beyond!" yelled Buzz, as he leaped off the roof.

Slinky jumped last. The search for Woody had begun!

Chapter Ten

Woody walked around Al's apartment in awe.

"I can't believe I had my own show!" he marvelled.

Jessie and Bullseye followed him around. Prospector watched from his box in the corner.

"Didn't ya know? Why, you're valuable property!" said Jessie.

"Oh, I wish the guys could see this. Hey howdy hey – that's me! I'm a yo-yo!" he said, picking up a yo-yo with his face on it and giving it a spin.

Next he walked over to 'Woody's Ball

Toss' and threw a ball, knocking out his front teeth. He put some coins in the Roundup bank and then played with the bubble machine. "What . . . you push the hat, and out comes . . . oh, out come bubbles! Clever."

Woody was getting used to the idea of being famous, and he liked it.

Bullseye popped the bubbles with his mouth as they came out. Jessie laughed.

Woody continued to explore, picking up a boot. He looked inside and a spring snake jumped out, smacking him in the face.

"Aha, I get it! There's a snake in my boot."

"Check this out, Woody," said Jessie.

She put on the Woody record player and it cranked out old Western music. Bullseye and Jessie began to dance around, and Woody joined them.

"Hop on, cowgirl!" said Woody, as he jumped onto the record player.

The record spun him around and he

jumped up to avoid the needle arm. Jessie joined him, jumping in time.

"Not bad," said Woody.

"Wooo-eee!" shouted Jessie. "Look at us! We're a complete set!"

"Now it's on to the museum," said Prospector.

"Museum?" asked Woody. He stopped short, causing all of them to trip over the needle of the record player. They flew across the room and landed in a heap on the shelf.

"What museum?" groaned Woody.

"We're being sold to the Konishi Toy Museum in Tokyo," explained Prospector.

"That's in Japan!" added Jessie.

"Japan? I can't go to Japan," said Woody, standing up and brushing the dust from his knees.

"What do you mean?" asked Jessie, straightening her pigtails.

"I gotta get back home to my owner – Andy," Woody explained. "Look, see?"

Woody raised his boot and pointed to

the name ANDY, which was etched on his sole.

"You still have an owner?" gasped Jessie.

"Oh, my goodness . . ." said Prospector, scratching his head.

"I can't do storage again. I won't go back into the dark," stated Jessie, pacing back and forth.

"Jessie, it's okay!" said Prospector, as Jessie started to wave her arms frantically.

"What's the matter? What's wrong with her?" asked Woody.

Jessie was crying in the corner. Prospector explained.

"Well, we've been waiting in storage for a long time, Woody." he said. "Waiting for you."

"Why me?" asked Woody.

"The museum's only interested in the collection if you're in it, Woody. Without you, we go back into storage. It's that simple."

"It's not fair!" cried Jessie. "How can you do this to us?"

"Hey, look." Woody put his arms up and backed away. "I'm sorry, but this is all a big mistake. See, I was in this yard sale and–"

"Yard sale?" said Prospector. "Why were you in a yard sale if you have an owner?"

"Oh, I wasn't supposed to be there," Woody explained.

"Is it because you're damaged? Did this Andy break you?" asked Prospector.

Woody cradled his arm in defence.

"Yes, but . . . no, no, no . . . it was an accident. He–"

"Sounds like he really loves you," snapped Jessie.

"It's not like that, okay!" shouted Woody. "I'm not going to any museum."

Suddenly the door creaked open.

"Al's coming," warned Prospector.

The Roundup Gang scrambled to their original positions.

Seconds later, Al was in the room. He bent down and grabbed a camera out of a box.

"Oh, ho, ho, ho . . . money, baby," laughed Al.

He pulled out Bullseye and Jessie and arranged them in front of the Roundup barn for a shot.

"Money, money, money. And now, the main attraction." He grabbed Woody from his case. But Woody's arm got caught on the stand and it tore off. Al noticed after he put Woody down on the stand.

"Aaaaah! His arm. Where's his arm?" Al yelled.

At last he saw it on the ground, grabbed it and tried to reattach it to Woody's shoulder.

"What am I going to do?" he asked. "Oh, I know."

Al put Woody down on a chair and then reached for the phone.

"Hey, it's me – Al – I got an emergency here," he barked into the phone. "It's got to be done tonight . . . all right, all right. But first thing in the morning. Grrr."

Al slammed the phone into its cradle and stomped out of the room, slamming the door behind him.

Woody came back to life.

"It's gone!" he said, horrified. "I can't believe it. My arm is completely gone!"

"Awright, come here," said Prospector. "Let me see that. Oh, it's just a popped seam. You should consider yourself lucky."

"Lucky! Are you shrink-wrapped?" said Woody. "I'm missing my arm!"

Jessie slumped in one corner. "Let him go. I'm sure his precious Andy is dying to play with a one-armed cowboy doll."

"Why, Jessie," reasoned Prospector, "you know he wouldn't last an hour out there in his condition. It's a dangerous world out there for a toy."

Chapter Eleven

Buzz leaped out of a pile of shrubs, sneaking between pools of streetlamp light. Finally, he took cover behind a post box at the corner. He looked back and motioned for the others to follow him.

Rex jumped out of the shrub first, camouflaged in leaves. As he ran to Buzz, all but one of the leaves fell to the ground.

"Oh!" he laughed. "This is just like when my invisibility shield wore off on Level 14 . . . I was completely exposed! Well! I made an earnest attempt to hide . . ."

Slinky, Potato Head and Hamm appeared next, scurrying along quickly.

Hamm tripped over a crack and his cork fell out. Coins clanged to the ground.

"Oow. Ooof. All right, nobody look till I get my cork back in," he cried.

"So then Zurg annihilated me with his ion blaster!" continued Rex.

"Oh, not the video game again," cried Mr Potato Head.

He popped his ears out so he wouldn't have to listen to Rex any more.

Buzz looked down at the map.

"Good work, men", he said. "One block down and only 19 more to go."

"Are we gonna do this all night? My parts are killing me," said Mr Potato Head.

Buzz waved his arm. "Come on, fellas. Did Woody give up when Sid had me strapped to a rocket?"

"No!" yelled the others.

"No! And did he give up when you threw him out of the back of that moving van?" asked Buzz.

"Oh, you had to bring that up," said Mr

Potato Head.

"We have a friend in need and until he's safe in Andy's room we will not rest. Now, let's move out!"

Buzz marched down the street and the other toys followed him.

Chapter Twelve

The sun rose over Andy's neighbourhood. Buzz and the gang were still on their way to the rescue.

"Hey, Buzz, can we slow down?" asked Hamm. "May I remind you that some of us are carrying over six dollars in change."

"Losing health units . . . must . . . rest," panted Rex.

Buzz stopped and waited for Hamm, Mr Potato Head, Rex and Slinky to catch up with him.

"Is everyone present and accounted for?" he asked.

"Not quite everyone," said Mr Potato

Head.

"Who's behind?" asked Buzz.

"Mine," said Slinky, whose back end was trailing far behind.

"Hey, guys!" said Hamm. "Why did the toys cross the road?"

"Not now, Hamm," said Buzz.

"Ooh! I love riddles. Why?" asked Rex.

"To get to the chicken on the other side!" Hamm answered.

He pointed. Al's Toy Barn was directly across the street. A giant chicken loomed in front.

"Hurray! The chicken!" shouted Rex.

Horns honked and a huge truck rumbled by, shooting an empty, crushed pop can towards the toys.

They ducked and scrambled out of the way. They stared at the busy road in front of them and shivered.

"Oh, well. We tried," said Rex, inching away from the street.

Buzz grabbed him by the tail.

"We'll have to cross," he said.

"You're not turning me into mashed potato!" said Mr Potato Head.

"I may not be a smart dog," said Slinky. "But I know what roadkill is!"

Buzz surveyed the scene. He spotted some orange cones and rubbed his hands together.

"I have an idea!" he said.

A minute later, each toy was securely under an orange cone at the edge of the road.

"Okay, here's our chance!" Buzz yelled. "Ready, set, go!"

The cones began to move across the street. Some cars sped in front of them.

"Drop!" warned Buzz.

All of the cones dropped.

"Go!" he shouted, when it was clear.

The cones hurried forward. Cars veered out of their way, and before long they were safely on the other side of the street.

"Good job, troops," said Buzz. "We're that much closer to Woody!"

The toys headed towards Al's Toy Barn.

But when they got close, they noticed a large sign that read CLOSED.

"Oh, no. It's closed!" cried Slinky.

"We're not preschool toys, Slinky. We can read," said Mr Potato Head.

"Shhh," said Rex. "Someone's coming."

The toys hid under a shopping trolley as a workman approached. He stepped on the black mat in front of the electronic doors and they slid open.

"Hey, Joe, you're late!" said another workman from inside the shop. "We've got a ton of toys to unload in the back. Let's get going."

"All right, I'm coming . . . I'm coming," said Joe.

The toys glanced at each other. Buzz nodded.

"All right, let's go," he said.

"But the sign says it's closed," said Rex.

Everyone ignored him and stood on the mat. Finally, Rex followed, shaking his head, but nothing happened. The doors remained closed.

"C'mon, open!" said Hamm. But still the doors stayed closed.

"No, no, no," said Buzz. "All together."

The toys watched as he counted off with his head.

"Now!" Buzz yelled, and all the toys jumped at once. When they landed, the doors whooshed open and they stepped inside.

Chapter Thirteen

Al's Toy Barn was huge. Thousands upon thousands of toys lined the walls.

"Whooaa, Nellie! How're we gonna find Woody in this place?" asked Slinky.

"Look for Al," said Buzz. "We find Al, we find Woody. Now, move out!"

The toys scattered in search of Woody.

Buzz turned a corner and came face to face with an entire aisle of Buzz Lightyear boxes. He stared in awe.

"Wow . . ."

He stepped forward to examine the toys more closely. A bright green glow captured his attention. A large cardboard sign read NOW WITH UTILITY BELT.

"I could use one of those," marvelled Buzz. He climbed to the top of the display case and reached for the belt. Before he was able to grab it, he spotted a giant pair of moon boots. He glanced up. Towering over him was the new Buzz Lightyear.

Meanwhile, Rex and Mr Potato Head were exploring a different aisle. Rex was ecstatic. He had found a book called *Defeat Zurg*. He couldn't stop talking about it. In fact, he was talking so much that Mr Potato Head popped his ears off so he wouldn't have to hear any more of his ramblings.

Suddenly, a red car swerved down the aisle towards Rex and Mr Potato Head. It screeched to a halt beside them, revealing its driver and passenger, Hamm and Slinky.

"Eh, I thought we could search in style," said Hamm.

"Nice going there, Hamm. So, how

'bout letting a toy with fingers drive?" said Mr Potato Head.

Hamm moved over and Mr Potato Head took the steering wheel. They drove off, ramming into the occasional shelf. Rex continued to babble on, but no one was paying attention.

Meanwhile, Andy's Buzz circled the New Buzz, sizing him up. He checked out his own reflection in New Buzz's shiny helmet glass.

"Am I really that fat?" he wondered.

Andy's Buzz spied the utility belt, and reached for it.

"Ho-yahhh!" yelled New Buzz, putting Andy's Buzz's arm in a lock.

He pointed to hundreds of other Buzz Lightyears still in their boxes.

"Oww! What are you doing?" complained Andy's Buzz.

"You're in direct violation of code six-four-oh-four-point-five, stating all Space Rangers are to be in hyper-sleep until awakened by authorized personnel," barked New Buzz in a stiff, computer-like voice.

"Oh, no," said Andy's Buzz.

New Buzz spun Andy's Buzz around, pushing him up against the display.

"You're breaking ranks, Ranger," he said.

New Buzz kicked Andy's Buzz's legs apart and kept him in an armlock. He opened his wrist communicator, distracted.

"Buzz Lightyear to Star Command. I've got an AWOL Space Ranger."

"Tell me I wasn't this deluded," complained Buzz, rolling his eyes.

"No back talk," warned New Buzz. "I have a laser and I will use it."

"You mean the laser that's a lightbulb?" teased Buzz, as he pressed the laser.

New Buzz gasped.

"Has your mind been melded? You could've killed me, Space Ranger. Or should I say, 'Traitor'?"

Buzz broke free.

"I don't have time for this," he said.

New Buzz raised his laser and aimed it at Buzz's head.

"Halt! I order you to halt!"

Buzz dropped from the podium to the floor. New Buzz jumped on his back, tackling him. They began to wrestle. Buzz got New Buzz into an armlock, and then pushed him into the Buzz Lightyear Pin Screen.

Chapter Fourteen

In another part of the shop, Rex was reading from his *Defeat Zurg* manual.

"Wow! It says how you defeat Zurg! Look!"

Rex placed the book in front of the windscreen so that everyone could see. But now no one could see where they were going. The car swerved and the other toys screamed.

"Rex! Watch it! Look out! We can't see!" they yelled.

The car was heading directly into a giant box of Superballs.

"Look out!" yelled Slinky.

The car grazed the side of the box and the Superballs spilled out, cascading wildly to the ground. It created a blizzard multicoloured rubber. Balls bounced off everything, including the car, Mr Potato Head and Hamm. Everyone yelled as the car spun around wildly.

Rex's *Defeat Zurg* manual flew out of the car.

"My source of power!" he yelled, jumping out of the car and racing after the book. It slid under a shelf, lost.

"Where'd it go? No! Come back!" He watched the car speed away. "Wait up! Dinosaur overboard!"

Rex chased after the car.

Meanwhile, Buzz had been overpowered by New Buzz. New Buzz shoved Buzz into an empty box and used the packaging wires to secure him.

"Ow!" said Buzz. "Listen to me! You're not really a Space Ranger! You're a toy! We're all toys! Do you hear me?"

New Buzz slid Buzz into a box and

closed the cardboard container.

"Well, that should hold you until the court-martial!"

"Let me go!" Buzz pleaded from the box.

New Buzz turned and left just as the other toys pulled up to him.

"Hey, Buzz," said Hamm.

New Buzz turned, took aim and fired his laser at the toys.

"Halt!" he shouted. "Who goes there?"

"Quit clowning around and get in the car," said Mr Potato Head.

"Buzz! Buzz! I know how to defeat Zurg!" said Rex.

"You do?" asked New Buzz.

"C'mon, I'll tell you about it on the way," said Rex.

Buzz watched from the shelf, horrified.

"No, no, guys! You've got the wrong Buzz!"

"Say, where'd ya get that cool belt, Buzz?" asked Hamm.

"Well, slotted pig, they're standard issue," said New Buzz.

He got in the car and they drove away. Buzz yelled from the box, but no one could hear him.

Chapter Fifteen

A flash went off, blinding Woody momentarily. He was propped up on his stand. The rest of the Roundup Gang was set up around him. *Flash, flash, flash* . . .

Al fanned through his new pictures with a huge smile on his face.

"It's like printing my own money!" he exclaimed.

The phone rang and Al picked it up.

"Yeah, what?" he shouted. "Oh, oh, Mr Konishi. I have the pictures right here. In fact, I'm in the car right now, on my way to the office to fax them to you. I'm going through the tunnel," he lied. "I'm breaking up."

He made some garbled sounds and then hung up the phone and hurried out.

As soon as Al left the room, Woody leaped from his stand.

"Oh, wow! Will you look at me! It's like I'm fresh out of the box!"

Woody admired his fixed arm. Someone had come to sew him up and clean him. He examined his new stitching.

"Will you look at this! Andy's gonna have a hard time ripping this!" Woody waved his new arm wildly in front of the other toys' faces. "Hello! Hi! Hello!"

Woody admired himself in the reflection of the cellophane of Prospector's box.

Jessie frowned and walked away.

"Great, now you can go," she said.

"Well, what a good idea," said Woody. He walked to the edge of the table and looked at the heating grate below. Bullseye nudged him from behind. Woody stared into his sad eyes.

"Woody, don't be mad at Jessie," said Prospector. "She's been through more than you know. Why not make amends before you leave, huh? It's the least you can do."

Woody sighed. "All right. But I don't know what good it'll do."

He went over to Jessie, who was hugging her knees and staring out of the window.

"Look, Jessie," he began, "I know you hate me for leaving, but I have to go back. I'm still Andy's toy. Well, if you knew him, you'd understand. You see, Andy's a real . . ."

"Let me guess," Jessie interrupted. "Andy's a real special kid, and to him, you're his buddy, his best friend; and when Andy plays with you, it's like, even though you're not moving, you feel like you're alive – because that's how he sees you."

"How did you know?" asked Woody. He was truly stunned.

Jessie stared at Woody. "Because Emily was just the same. She was my whole world."

Jessie started to cry. She buried her head in her hands. Her voice came out muffled.

"You never forget kids like Emily, or Andy, but they forget you," she sobbed.

"Jessie, I . . . I didn't know," said Woody.

"Just go," she said.

Woody reluctantly slumped off. He jumped off the windowsill to the floor and walked back to the grate where the Prospector and Bullseye stood. Woody opened the grate and stared down at the ventilation shaft. He glanced back at Jessie.

"How long will it last, Woody?" asked Prospector. "Do you really think Andy is going to take you to college? Or on his honeymoon? Andy's growing up and there's nothing you can do about it. It's your choice, Woody. You can go back, or you can stay with us and be adored by children for generations. You'll live forever."

Woody let go of the grate and spun around.

"Who am I to break up the Roundup Gang?" he said.

Bullseye licked his hand, and Prospector smiled. Woody and Jessie grinned at each other.

Chapter Sixteen

The toys rummaged through the desk and drawers in Al's office.

"Woody, are you in here?" asked Hamm.

"Woody?" they called.

Rex approached New Buzz.

"You see, all along we thought that the way into Zurg's fortress was through the main gate," he explained. "But in fact, the secret entrance is to the left, hidden in the shadows."

New Buzz turned.

"To the left and in the shadows," he repeated. "Got it."

They heard Al enter the office and they hid.

Al turned on his fax machine as he talked into his mobile phone.

"Yeah, there was a big pileup, but I don't want to bore you with the details. Now, let me confirm your fax number. All right, slower. That's a lot of numbers. I got it."

"It's him," whispered Slinky.

"The chicken man," said Hamm.

"Funny, he doesn't look like poultry," said New Buzz.

"That's the kidnapper, all right," said Slinky.

"An agent of Zurg if I ever saw one," said New Buzz.

"And the pièce de résistance," Al said, as he slid a picture of Woody through the fax. "I promise the collection will be the crown jewel of your museum!"

The photo went through the machine and popped out on the other side, falling to the floor near where the toys hid.

"Woody!" they gasped.

"Now that I have your attention, imagine we added another zero to the price, huh? What? Yes? Yes! You've got a deal!" Al yelled. "I'll be on the next flight to Japan!"

"He's selling Woody to a toy museum," whispered Mr Potato Head.

"In Japan!" said Rex.

New Buzz pushed everyone into Al's bag.

"Into the poultry man's cargo unit," he ordered. "He'll lead us to Zurg. Move, move, move!"

Al laughed like a maniac.

"I'm gonna be rich! Rich! Rich!" he bellowed, picking up his bag as the last of the toys slipped in.

Rex's tail dangled out of the back of the bag.

Chapter Seventeen

Back at the toyshop, Buzz had managed to shift his box sideways on the shelf. With each shove against the plastic, he moved another inch. He teetered over the edge and finally dropped to the floor.

Buzz kicked open the bottom of the box, then struggled with the arm restraints. He jerked his right arm hard and broke free. He untied the rest of his body and then crawled out of the box, kicking it in disgust.

Buzz heard Al coming down the aisle and hid. He peered around the corner after Al went past, and noticed Rex's tail sticking out of the back of the bag that Al carried. Buzz raced down a parallel aisle, trying to catch up with his friends. He was almost at the door when he slipped on some loose Superballs left over from the crash. Buzz stumbled forward, waving his arms wildly to try to get his balance. As he staggered, he saw Al leave the shop.

Buzz recovered quickly and crawled up the display case. Swinging like a gymnast, he jumped onto a trampoline.

When he had bounced high enough, Buzz dived for the closing electric doors in desperation . . . and smacked right into the glass.

"Ooph!" yelled Buzz.

He jumped up and down on the electric sensor on the doormat, but he wasn't heavy enough and the door just wouldn't budge.

Buzz looked around and spotted a large stack of boxes by the door. He kicked the bottom box out, causing the entire pile to topple over. The door opened with their weight and Buzz ran towards it. He raced out of the door, chasing after Al.

Buzz didn't notice that when the electronic doors closed, the top of one of the boxes ripped open. Zurg crawled out, and then whipped his head towards Buzz. His red eyes glowered and his claws clenched as he watched Buzz. His deep mechanical voice growled, "Destroy Buzz Lightyear . . . Destroy Buzz Lightyear."

Set free, Zurg followed Buzz's trail.

Chapter Eighteen

The toys heard Al cut the engine. He got out of the car, slamming the door behind him.

"He didn't take the bag!" said Rex, as he watched from inside.

New Buzz hopped over Rex and jumped out.

"No time to lose," he said.

He tried the door handle, but couldn't get it open.

They all watched Al get into the lift.

"He's ascending in the vertical transporter," said New Buzz. He opened his wings and grabbed hold of Rex and

Mr Potato Head. "All right, everyone! Hang on! We're going to blast through the roof!"

"Uh, Buzz," said Rex.

"To infinity and beyond!" boomed New Buzz.

"What are you, insane?" asked Mr Potato Head. He noticed the car door lock next to the window, and ran up Rex's back so he could reach it. "Stand still, Godzilla," he said.

Mr Potato Head strained to lift the lock. New Buzz scratched his head and leaned against the electric window switch.

"I don't understand. Somehow my fuel cells have gone dry . . ."

Ka-chunk! Suddenly the lock popped open, tearing off Mr Potato Head's arms. He sailed through the air and bounced off Slinky's head.

"Ahhh!" he yelled.

He finally landed upside down in the cup holder.

The car door opened and New Buzz ran

out. He watched through the glass doors as the lift needle stopped at the penthouse.

"Blast!" cried New Buzz. "He's on Level 23."

"How are we gonna get up there?" asked Slinky.

Rex looked up. "Maybe if we find some balloons, we could float to the top . . ."

The others looked at him in surprise.

"Are you kidding?" asked Mr Potato Head. "I say we stack ourselves up, push the intercom and pretend we're delivering a pizza!"

"How about a ham sandwich?" asked Hamm. He glanced at Mr Potato Head and Slinky. "With fries and a hot dog?"

"What about me?" asked Rex.

"Eh, you can be the toy that comes with the meal," shrugged Hamm.

"Troops! Over here," said New Buzz.

They all turned to see New Buzz taking the cover off an air vent.

"Just like you said, Lizard Man – in the

shadows, to the left. Okay, let's move!"

The toys followed New Buzz into the duct. New Buzz spoke into his wrist communicator.

"Mission Log – have infiltrated enemy territory without detection and are making our way through the bowels of Zurg's fortress."

Hamm turned to the others.

"You know, I think that Buzz aisle went to his head," he whispered.

The others nodded, but they all followed New Buzz through the shaft.

Soon after, they came to a crossroads. Slinky looked in both directions.

"Oh, no . . . which way do we go?" he asked.

"This way," said New Buzz, running forward.

"What makes you so sure?" asked Mr Potato Head.

"I'm Buzz Lightyear. I'm always sure!"

Before anyone could respond, a noise echoed throughout the duct.

"We've been detected," said New Buzz. "The walls! They're closing in."

New Buzz grabbed Mr Potato Head and lifted him overhead.

"Quick! Help me prop up Vegetable Man, or we're done for!" he said.

"Put me down, you moron!" cried Mr Potato Head.

"Hey, guys, look! It's not the walls, it's the elevator," said Rex.

He pointed to a different duct, where they caught sight of the lift heading down.

They walked to the lift shaft and peered up. New Buzz put on his suction cup gloves and reeled out a line and hook.

"Come on," he said, handing out the line. "We've got no time to lose. Everyone grab hold."

"Huh?" asked the others.

"Hey, er, Buzz?" said Hamm. "Why don't we just take the elevator?"

New Buzz began to scale the walls.

"They'll be expecting that," he

explained.

Meanwhile, a weary and frustrated Buzz made it to the front of Al's apartment building. He noticed a trail of footprints in the soft grass, leading to the vent. He ducked down and followed the trail.

Chapter Nineteen

Al paced back and forth in his living room, yelling into his phone once more.

"To overnight six packages to Japan is how much? What? That's in yen, right? Dollars? Doh! You are deliberately taking advantage of people in a hurry, you know that? All right, I don't . . . I'll do it! All right, fine!"

He stacked a pile of boxes onto a cart with wheels and headed out of the door with it.

"I'll have the stuff waiting in the lobby and you'd better be here in 15 minutes, because I have a plane to catch. Do you hear me?"

The members of the Roundup Gang were packed into their boxes too. But they weren't being shipped to Japan. They were going on the plane with Al in his carry-on case.

When Al left the apartment, Woody, Jessie and Bullseye sat up.

"Woo-hoo!" yelled Jessie. "We're finally going! Can you believe it?"

Bullseye sniffed excitedly and then snuggled into his thick foam packaging.

Prospector chuckled. "That's custom-fitted foam insulation you'll be riding in, Bullseye. First-class stuff, all the way!"

"You know what?" said Woody. "I'm actually excited about this. I mean it. I really am."

Jessie jumped next to Woody, and they began to square dance.

"Yee-haw! Swing yer partner, doh-see-doh," she sang. "Look at you, dancin' cowboy!"

Bullseye clapped his hooves. Prospector glided his box back and forth.

"Look! I'm doing the box step!" he cried.

Chapter Twenty

Thock, thock, thock. New Buzz climbed the wall slowly, pulling the others behind him.

Hamm grunted. He tilted and some of his change began to drop out of his coin slot.

"Uh-oh . . . hey, heads up down there," he called.

"Whoa! Pork bellies are falling," said Slinky.

Some coins landed on Mr Potato Head's face.

"Hey," he yelled. "Not much farther, Buzz?" he asked, hopefully.

"My arms can't hold on much longer," complained Rex.

The lift shaft shuddered, causing Rex to slide down the line. He bumped into the other toys and pushed them down with him. In the end, they were all desperately clinging to the bottom of the line.

"Buzz, help!" called Slinky.

"Too . . . heavy . . ." panted New Buzz. He couldn't hold on for much longer! Suddenly, he had an idea. "What was I thinking? My antigravity servos!" He pushed a button on his utility belt.

"Hurry up, Buzz," said Hamm.

"Hang tight, everyone," said New Buzz. "I'm going to let go of the wall."

"What!" the toys cried.

"He wouldn't," said Mr Potato Head.

"One," said Buzz.

"He would," said Hamm.

"Two," he called.

"For the love of . . . no!"

"Three," called New Buzz.

He pushed off from the wall and went

into his flying pose. He looked up, his fist jutting forward. They were frozen in space for a second. And then . . . they plummeted down, landing on the top of the lift as it was rising.

"To infinity and beyond," called New Buzz, unaware that his attempt at flying had failed.

The lift began to slow down.

"Approaching new destination. Re-engaging gravity," New Buzz said.

The others looked at each other and rolled their eyes. The lift stopped next to the airshaft of the 23rd floor. New Buzz leaped into the vent and scanned the area.

"Area secure," he reported to the others.

They groaned and panted as they climbed into the vent.

"It's okay, troops. The antigravity sickness will wear off," said Buzz. "Now . . . let's move!"

"Remind me to glue his helmet shut when we get back," Mr Potato Head whispered to Hamm.

Once inside the vent, New Buzz spoke into his wrist communicator again. "Have reached Zurg's command deck, but no sign of him or his wooden captive."

Suddenly, Woody's voice echoed through the chambers.

"That's Woody!" said Slinky.

The toys turned and ran down the duct. They reached the grate to Al's apartment in a few seconds, and they tried to peer through.

Woody was being tickled by Jessie, but his friends could only hear his voice.

"I'm begging you! No more! I'm begging you, stop. Please!" he shouted.

"Buzz, can you see what's going on?" asked Mr Potato Head.

New Buzz lifted one of Mr Potato Head's eyes up to the slats in the vent.

"What's happening?" he asked.

Mr Potato Head gasped.

"It's horrible!" he cried. "They're torturing him!"

"What are we going to do, Buzz?" asked Rex.

"Use your head," said New Buzz.

The toys grabbed Rex and aimed his head at the door. Using him as a battering ram, they scrambled forward.

"But I don't want to use my head," cried Rex.

"CHARGE!" they all yelled.

Woody had left the grate unscrewed, so the stampeding toys caused the grate to fall down even before they reached it. Unable to stop, they all sped into the room, passing the Roundup Gang and smashing into the far wall.

Everyone yelled.

"What's going on here?" asked Prospector.

"Guys!" cried Woody. "Hey, how did you find me?"

"We're here to spring you, Woody," explained Slinky.

Andy's toys rushed towards the Roundup Gang.

"Hold it, now! Hey, you don't understand! These are my friends," said Woody.

"Yeah, we're his friends," said Rex, puffing his chest out.

"Well, not you – them," said Woody, nodding at the Roundup Gang.

Chapter Twenty-One

Slinky quickly circled around Jessie and Bullseye, tying them up with his coils.

"Hey," said Jessie.

"Grab Woody and let's go," said Slinky.

New Buzz ran to Woody, picked him up and started to carry him off.

"Fellas, hold it!" Woody protested. "Hey, Buzz – put me down."

"They're stealing him!" cried Jessie.

The toys rushed towards the vent, but Andy's Buzz was blocking it.

"Hold it right there!" he said.

"Buzz?" said Woody and Andy's other toys.

"You again?" asked New Buzz.

Buzz looked up at Woody, who was still in New Buzz's arms.

"Woody, thank goodness you're all right," he said.

"Buzz, what's going on?" asked Woody.

New Buzz dropped Woody.

"Hold on a minute," he said. "I am Buzz Lightyear, and I'm in charge of this detachment."

"No, I'm Buzz Lightyear," said Buzz to the others.

"So who's the real Buzz?" asked Woody.

"I am," they both said.

New Buzz turned to the others.

"Don't let this imposter fool you," he told them. "He's probably been trained by Zurg himself to mimic my every move."

Buzz reached over and popped New Buzz's helmet open. New Buzz spluttered and gasped for air, falling to the ground.

While New Buzz faltered, Buzz calmly lifted his foot and showed everyone the ANDY written on the sole.

"I had a feeling it was you, Buzz," said Slinky. "My front end just had to catch up to my back end."

Rex looked from one Buzz to the other. "You know, now that I really look I can see the difference."

New Buzz managed to close his helmet and stand up.

"Will someone please explain what's going on?" he asked.

"It's all right, Space Ranger," said Buzz. "It's a code five-four-six."

"You mean it's a . . ." said New Buzz.

"Yes," said Buzz.

"And he's a . . ." said New Buzz.

"Yes," said Buzz.

New Buzz rushed over to Woody and bowed down on one knee.

"Your Majesty," he said.

Woody looked down, confused. Buzz took his arm.

"Woody, you're in danger here," he said. "We need to leave now."

"Al's selling you to a toy museum in

Japan!" said Rex.

"I know, it's okay," said Woody, pulling away. "I actually want to go."

"What? Are you crazy?" asked Mr Potato Head.

"The thing is," explained Woody, "I'm a rare Sheriff Woody doll, and these guys are my Roundup Gang."

He motioned to Jessie, Bullseye and Prospector, who waved.

"What are you talking about?" asked Mr Potato Head.

"*Woody's Roundup*! It's this great old TV show, and I was the star!"

Woody clicked the remote and the TV and VCR turned on with the show playing in the middle of an episode.

"See, now look . . . look at me! See, that's me!" said Woody.

On the screen, the TV Woody was riding the TV Bullseye towards a cliff. TV Jessie fell off and they caught her.

Andy's toys watched in amazement.

"This is weirdin' me out," said Hamm.

"Buzz, it was a national phenomenon," Woody explained. "And there was all this merchandise that just got packed up. You should see it. There was a record player, a cereal box and a yo-yo. Buzz, I was a yo-yo."

"Was?" questioned Mr Potato Head.

Buzz pulled Woody aside.

"Woody, stop this nonsense and let's go," he said.

"I can't go. I can't abandon these guys. Without me the set's incomplete. They'll go back into storage – maybe forever. They need me to get into the museum."

Buzz raised his voice. "You – Are – A – Toy! You're not a collector's item. You are a child's plaything."

"For how much longer?" reasoned Woody. "One more rip and Andy's done with me. What do I do then, Buzz, huh? You tell me."

"Woody, the point is being there for Andy when he needs us," said Buzz. "You taught me that. That's why we came all this way to get you."

"Well, you wasted your time," sighed Woody.

Buzz and Woody stared at each other for a minute.

Buzz turned towards the grate.

"Let's go, everyone," he said.

"What about Woody?" asked Slinky.

"He's not coming with us," said Buzz.

"But, but, Andy's coming home tonight," said Rex.

"Then we'd better make sure we're there waiting for him," said Buzz.

Buzz held the vent open for the rest of Andy's toys and New Buzz. They glanced at Woody sadly before filing out and disappearing into the darkness. Buzz paused and looked at Woody.

"I don't have a choice, Buzz," said Woody, shrugging his shoulders. "This museum . . . it's my only chance."

"To do what, Woody?" asked Buzz. "Watch children from behind glass? Some life."

He jumped into the vent and closed the grate behind him.

Woody stared at the closed grate as the Roundup Gang toys approached him.

"Good going, Woody. I thought they'd never leave," said Prospector.

Woody wandered over to the TV to watch the end of the episode. The TV Woody was singing. The song trickled in through the grate, and Andy's toys paused to listen for a moment.

On the TV screen, a shy little boy was pushed onto the stage. He slowly approached TV Woody. The boy hugged TV Woody with all his might.

Woody looked down at the sole of his shoe. He scratched away the new paint until the name ANDY showed through. Woody got up.

"What am I doing?" he said.

He ran past the Roundup Gang, heading straight for the vent.

"W-Woody? Where are you going?" asked Prospector.

"You're right, Prospector," said Woody. "I can't stop Andy from growing up, but I wouldn't miss it for the world!"

"No!" gasped Jessie and Prospector.

"Buzz! Buzz!" yelled Woody, running through the vent.

Both Buzzes turned.

"Yes?" they asked.

"Wait! I'm coming with you!" Woody said.

Andy's toys cheered.

"Wait for me," said Woody. "I'll be back in just a second."

He turned on his boot heel and headed back towards Al's apartment.

Chapter Twenty-Two

Woody rushed back into Al's apartment.

"Hey, you guys!" he called to the Roundup Gang. "Come with me!"

Jessie, Bullseye and Prospector stared at Woody in surprise.

"Look," said Woody. "I know I won't be played with forever, but Buzz is right. Today I still have Andy, and today I know he'd play with all of us."

"Woody, I . . . I don't know," stuttered Jessie.

"Wouldn't you give anything just to have one more day with Emily?" asked Woody. "Well, here's your chance! Come on! Take it!" Woody glanced at Bullseye. "Are you with me?" he asked.

Bullseye eagerly licked Woody's face.

"Good boy," Woody laughed. "Good boy. Prospector, how about you?"

Woody turned to Prospector's box, but it was empty. Woody's eyes opened wide with terror. Prospector had slammed the grate shut and was using his plastic pick like a power tool to spin the screws tight.

Jessie gasped.

"You're outta your box?" asked Woody, horrified.

"I tried reasoning with you, Woody," said Prospector. He finished tightening the screws and walked back to his box. "But you keep forcing me to take extreme measures."

Woody started to protest, but Prospector raised his hand to silence him.

"Look, we have an eternity to spend together in the museum. Let's not start off by pointing fingers, shall we?"

"Prospector! This isn't fair," said Jessie.

"Fair," said Prospector. "I'll tell you what's not FAIR. Spending a lifetime on a dime-store shelf, watching every other toy be sold. Well, finally my waiting has paid off, and no hand-me-down cowboy doll is gonna screw it up for me now!"

Prospector flung his box into the special packing case and then climbed in himself.

Woody ran to the vent, pulling on the grate.

"Help! Help! Buzz! Guys!" he screamed.

"It's too late," called Prospector. "That silly Buzz Lightweight can't help you."

"His name is Buzz Lightyear!" shouted Woody.

"Whatever," said Prospector, closing the lid of his box.

Andy's toys raced down the vent towards the grate. They struggled to open it, but it wouldn't budge.

"It's stuck," called Woody.

The two Buzzes began slamming into it.

"Should I use my head?" offered Rex.

The lock on Al's apartment door began to rattle. Jessie and Bullseye jumped into their cases as the door creaked open. Woody had no choice but to join the rest of the Roundup Gang.

"Ah! Look at the time. I'm gonna be late," growled Al.

Andy's toys watched in horror as Woody was taken away.

"Quick! To the elevator," cried Buzz.

The toys raced down the duct. But they were in for a very nasty surprise.

Chapter Twenty-Three

Zurg was riding on top of the lift.

"All too easy," he muttered, as Buzz Lightyear came into view.

"It's Zurg!" yelled Rex. "Watch out, he's got an ion blaster."

Zurg fired at New Buzz, who jumped into action. New Buzz leaped over Zurg and moved swiftly to avoid all of his assaults.

Zurg whipped his body around and fired his ion balls. *Pop, pop, pop.*

New Buzz ducked for cover behind a generator box.

Meanwhile, Al got into the lift with the

Roundup Gang in tow.

As the lift descended, New Buzz and Zurg began to fist fight.

"Quick, get on," cried Buzz.

The toys jumped onto the roof of the lift. They watched New Buzz's struggle. Zurg lifted him overhead and threw him to the ground.

"Surrender, Buzz Lightyear. I have won," boomed Zurg.

"I'll never give in. You killed my father," said New Buzz.

"No, Buzz . . . I am your father," said Zurg.

"NO-O-O!" screamed New Buzz.

Rex scrambled down from the top of the lift and ran up behind Zurg.

"Buzz, you could have defeated Zurg all along. You just need to believe in yourself!" said Rex.

Zurg raised his blaster to New Buzz's head.

"Prepare to die!" shouted Zurg.

"Ahh, I can't look," said Rex, covering

his eyes.

As he turned away, his tail knocked Zurg off balance. Zurg fell, rolled to the edge of the lift shaft and then tumbled down, plunging into the darkness.

"AAHHHH!" yelled Zurg.

Rex peered over the edge of the elevator shaft.

"I did it!" he cried. "I finally defeated Zurg!"

New Buzz joined Rex and looked down.

"Father?" said New Buzz.

Meanwhile, Slinky dangled down into the lift and managed to unlock Al's case, freeing Woody. They grabbed hold of each other as the lift touched down in the lobby. Slinky pulled Woody from one end, but Prospector pulled from the other, forcing Woody back into the case.

Al exited the lift, taking Woody with him. The toys followed and watched him get into his car.

"How are we gonna get him now?" asked Rex.

Mr Potato Head pointed to an idling Pizza Planet truck.

"Pizza, anyone?" he asked.

Everyone smiled and headed towards the truck.

Buzz noticed New Buzz falling behind.

"Are you coming?" he asked.

New Buzz was carrying a lifeless Zurg in his arms.

"No," he said sadly. "I must bury my father, and fill out the proper forms."

They waved goodbye, and New Buzz walked back to Al's Toy Barn.

The toys climbed into the truck and Buzz took control of the situation.

"Slink, take the pedals. Rex, you navigate." He slid a stack of pizza boxes under the steering wheel. "Hamm and Potato, operate the levers and knobs."

Inside the truck, three tiny green aliens hung from the rear-view mirror.

"Strangers, from the outside," they said.

"Oh, no!" moaned Buzz.

Rex pointed. "He's at the red light. We can catch him."

"Maximum power, Slink," Buzz ordered.

Slinky pushed on the accelerator with all his might. The truck wouldn't budge. On the dashboard, Rex peered through the windscreen.

"It turned green," he exclaimed. "Hurry up!"

"Why won't it go?" asked Buzz.

The aliens pointed to the gearstick.

"Use the wand of power," they said.

Standing on top of Hamm, Mr Potato Head struggled to get the car into gear. He jammed the gears hard and the truck sped forward.

"Ahh!" yelled Rex, as the truck hit a row of orange cones.

"Rex, which way?" asked Old Buzz.

"Right. I mean left. No, no, right . . . I mean *your* right!" said Rex.

The truck sped down the street, swerving wildly. Al's car turned.

"There he is!" shouted Rex. "He's

turning left!"

Buzz cranked the steering wheel and the truck cut across three lanes of traffic. The aliens swung on their string and flew across the car, heading out of the window. Mr Potato Head leaned out and grabbed them just in time.

"Buzz! Go right! To the right! Right!" shouted Rex.

The truck turned again, and Mr Potato Head and the aliens whipped safely back into the truck.

"You saved our lives!" chanted the aliens. "We are forever in your debt."

Mr Potato Head slapped his forehead and groaned.

Chapter Twenty-Four

The toys sped into the airport, parking in the unloading area.

"There he is!" said Buzz, pointing to Al. He was checking in and handing his case to the ticket agent.

The toys sneaked up behind Al, hidden in a pet carrier.

"Once we get through, we just need to find that case," said Buzz.

The pet carrier was checked, and the toys rode down the conveyor belt with the bags. When the carrier tumbled onto the lower conveyor belt, it burst open, freeing the toys.

Slinky spied Al's case first.

"There it is!" he yelled, pointing to the right.

"No, there's the case!" said Hamm, pointing to the left.

"You take that one, and we'll take this one," said Buzz.

Hamm, Rex and Mr Potato Head ran to the case on the left. They unzipped it, only to find a jumble of camera equipment.

Buzz chased after the case on the right and kicked open the latch.

"Okay, Woody, let's go!" he called.

Buzz reached into the case and opened it, only to be punched and knocked off the belt by Prospector.

Prospector climbed out and waved his plastic pick at Buzz.

"Take that, space toy!" he yelled.

Suddenly Woody popped up beside Prospector and grabbed him in a headlock.

"Hey! No one does that to my friend!" he said.

In their struggle, both toys fell out of the case. Prospector slashed Woody's arm with his pick, and it ripped open once more.

"Your choice, Woody!" growled Prospector. "You can go to Japan together . . . or in pieces! If he fixed you once, he can fix you again! Now, get in the box."

"Never," said Woody.

Prospector raised his pick to land one final blow, when he was blinded by light.

Snap, snap, snap. Andy's toys shot Prospector with the cameras, distracting him with the flashing.

"Gotcha!" yelled Buzz, grabbing Prospector.

"Fools!" sputtered Prospector. "Children will destroy you! You'll be ruined! Forgotten! Thrown away . . . spending eternity decomposing in some rotten landfill!"

"Well, Stinky Pete, I think it's time you learned the true meaning of *playtime*," said Woody. "Right over there, guys."

"No!" gasped Prospector, as they stuffed him into a child's rucksack. "You can't do this to me! Noooo!"

"Hi!" said one of the dolls inside.

Prospector looked up, startled. He turned the other way to find another doll.

"You'll like Amy," said a third doll. "She's an artist."

Prospector was surrounded by six dolls in various states of design. Scattered in the bag with them were crayons, scissors and paintbrushes.

Prospector screamed as the case made its way along the conveyor belt. Buzz and Woody waved at him.

"Happy trails, Prospector," called Woody.

"Hey, Woody," said Hamm. "We can't get Jessie out!"

The case was approaching the end of the conveyer belt, and Jessie was still stuck inside.

"Woody! Help!" she yelled.

Still in the case, Jessie plummeted

down a steep belt ramp. The toys watched in horror as a baggage handler closed the case, loaded it onto a luggage cart and drove off.

Woody whistled and Bullseye galloped forward. Woody and Buzz jumped up on his back.

"Ride like the wind, Bullseye," Woody yelled.

Bullseye reared up and took off in pursuit of Jessie.

"Yee-ha! Giddy-up!" said Woody.

The three raced up next to the moving luggage cart. Woody jumped onto the cart and struggled with the case that contained Jessie. The baggage handlers approached and Woody had to freeze, watching in horror as the case was loaded onto the plane.

Woody sneaked onto the plane. He found the case and opened it, finding Jessie on top of the foam.

"Excuse me, ma'am . . . but I believe you're on the wrong flight," he said with a smile.

"Woody!" yelled Jessie.

"Come on, Jess. It's time to take you home." Woody hugged Jessie.

"But I'm a girl toy," said Jessie.

"Nonsense," said Woody. "Andy will love you. Besides, he's got a little sister."

"He does?" said Jessie. "Well, why didn't you say so? Let's go."

Woody grabbed Jessie's arm and pulled her out of the case. The two ran behind a suitcase, hiding from the baggage handler.

Before they could escape, though, the doors closed.

Buzz and Bullseye stared in disbelief from the runway below.

"What are we gonna do?" gasped Jessie.

"Come on! Over there!"

Woody pointed to some light leaking in from the other end of the cargo hold. They ran over and peered through the opening at the landing gear below.

"Are you sure about this?" asked Jessie.

"Yes, now go," said Woody.

He used his pull string like a lasso and secured it around a bolt protruding from the landing gear. Woody and Jessie swung down, landing beside Buzz on Bullseye's back.

"Yeee-haaa!" yelled Woody. He disconnected his pull string just as the plane picked up speed, escaping just in time.

"We did it!" yelled Jessie. "That was definitely Woody's finest hour!"

"Nice ropin', cowboy," said Buzz.

He handed Woody his hat, which had fallen off earlier.

"Let's go home," said Woody.

Chapter Twenty-Five

The Davis van pulled up to the house and stopped. Andy jumped out and ran towards the front door. He burst into his bedroom and jumped onto his chair, searching his shelf for Woody. But all he could find were some dusty old books.

Disappointed, he turned and looked around the room. On his bed he saw WELCOME HOME, ANDY spelled out on Etch. Surrounding Etch were all of his toys, plus Jessie and Bullseye. Overjoyed, Andy jumped down from the chair and picked up Woody, Jessie and Bullseye.

"Oh, wow!" he gasped. "Thanks, Mum!"

Andy played with his toys.

"Woody and the cowgirl fly across the Snake River Canyon," said Andy. "Oh, no! They're attacked by a ferocious dinosaur. Rooaar!"

Andy picked up Rex and smashed him into Bullseye.

"Help, help, somebody! A dinosaur's eatin' my horse!" Andy said, in Jessie's voice.

"Buzz Lightyear flies in to save the day," Andy continued. "Take that, dinosaur," he said, in Buzz's voice.

"Andy, breakfast is ready," called Mrs Davis.

"Okay, Mum. Be there in a second," yelled Andy.

Before Andy left, he wrote his name on the sole of Jessie's boot and Bullseye's hoof. Then he ran out.

As soon as he left, Jessie grinned and showed her boot to Bullseye.

"Yee-ha!" she said. "We're part of a family again, huh, Bullseye?"

"Ahem," said Buzz, approaching Jessie. "I'd just like to say that your hair . . . it's a lovely shade of . . . yarn . . . uh, I gotta go," he spluttered, turning away.

Jessie lassoed Buzz with her pull string and pulled him closer.

"Well, ain't you the sweetest space toy I ever met!" she said.

Woody came up behind them.

"Buzz has a girlfriend. Buzz has a girlfriend," he teased.

Buzz blushed.

Jessie put her hands on her hips.

"He does? Who is she? Well, she's gonna have to get past me!"

Meanwhile, the three aliens looked adoringly at Mr Potato Head.

"You saved our lives," they chanted. "We are eternally grateful."

"You saved their lives?" asked Mrs Potato Head. "My hero! I'm so proud of you." She gave him a kiss. "And they're so adorable," she said, glancing at the aliens. "Let's adopt them."

"Daddy!" said the aliens.

"Oh, no!" said Mr Potato Head. He slapped his hand to his forehead and fell backwards. His parts came loose as he landed on his back.

Meanwhile, Hamm was playing the video game.

"Hey, Rex, can you give me a hand over here? I need your magic touch," he said.

"I don't need to play. I've lived it," sighed Rex.

Hamm turned off the game. Al's Toy Barn advert flashed onto the screen.

"Welcome to Al's Toy Barn," said a sobbing TV Al. "We've got the lowest prices in town. Everything for a buck, buck, buck!"

Hamm and Rex watched intently.

"Crime doesn't pay!" Hamm said to the TV.

Woody showed Bo his arm, which Andy had mended with orange thread.

"Andy did a good job, huh? What do you think?"

"I like it," said Bo. "It makes you look tough."

Wheezy waddled over, squeaking.

"Wheezy, you're fixed!" said Woody.

"Oh, yeah," he said. "Mr Shark looked in the toy box and found me an extra squeaker."

"And how do you feel?" asked Woody.

"I feel swell . . . in fact, I think I feel a song coming on!"

Mr Microphone tossed Wheezy his mike.

Woody left the festivities and walked over to the far windowsill. Buzz joined him.

"You still worried?" asked Buzz.

"About Andy? No," said Woody. "It'll be fun while it lasts."

"I'm proud of you, cowboy," said Buzz, patting him on the back.

"Besides," said Woody, "when it all ends, I'll have old Buzz Lightyear to keep me company . . . for infinity and beyond!"

Buzz and Woody laughed, and joined their friends.

Disney · PIXAR

WALL·E

THE BOOK OF THE FILM

Adapted by Irene Trimble

Based on the screenplay by
Andrew Stanton & Jim Reardon

Parragon

Bath · New York · Singapore · Hong Kong · Cologne · Delhi · Melbourne

First published by Parragon in 2008
Parragon
Queen Street House
4 Queen Street
Bath BA1 1HE, UK

Copyright © 2008 Disney Enterprises, Inc. and Pixar
All rights reserved. No part of this publication may be reproduced, stored in a retrieval system or transmitted, in any form or by any means, electronic, mechanical, photocopying, recording or otherwise, without the prior permission of the copyright holder.

ISBN 978-1-4075-1847-3

PROLOGUE

In the vast regions of outer space, beyond the twinkling lights of a million stars, a murky, smog-covered Earth floats lonely and silent. The deepest oceans are all but dried and gone. What had once been blue sky is now a dust-choked brown that can still look almost golden when sunlight filters through it.

Beneath the thick atmosphere that surrounds the planet, mountains still rise up through the haze, and once-great cities filled with vacant, crumbling buildings share the landscape with towers of trash, neatly cubed and stacked as far as the eye can see. Only one thing moves along this bleak twenty-ninth-century skyline.

Day in and day out, for more than seven

hundred years, he has worked to clean up the mess left by humankind. The scouring sands that sweep along the avenues seldom deter him as he thrusts his shovel-like hands into the heaps of trash and scoops it into the compacting unit in his chest. Once full, he closes the squeaky doors of his front panel, shakes a little, and produces yet another perfect cube ready to be stacked.

This is his directive.

It is what he has been programmed to do.

His name is WALL•E: Waste Allocation Load Lifter, Earth class.

He is a robot.

He is dented, dirty, and rusted . . .

And he is about to change the entire world.

CHAPTER 1

"Chirrrp!" A little cockroach jumped happily onto WALL•E's shoulder. As the toxic winds began to pick up speed, WALL•E and his only companion motored bouncily towards home. WALL•E's treads were wearing thin, and the cockroach held on bravely as they crossed the rough terrain.

Over miles of desolate waste, WALL•E saw buildings and highways and rolled across the remains of broken bridges. Everything was branded with the same logo: BUY-N-LARGE. BnL had its stamp on everything. The megasuperstore had once overseen almost all operations on the planet.

As WALL•E hurried onwards, he rolled over an old newspaper. TOO MUCH TRASH! EARTH

COVERED! BnL CEO DECLARES GLOBAL EMERGENCY! the headline proclaimed. WALL•E did not notice.

He passed a salvage yard full of other rusted WALL•E units, shut down long ago. The cockroach watched eagerly as WALL•E stopped to examine something of interest on one of the old units – its treads.

The treads were thick bands of rubber, built to protect the WALL•E units' metallic wheels like giant tyres. This old unit's treads were in much better shape than WALL•E's.

WALL•E quickly swapped his old pair for the newer ones as the cockroach chirped and jumped excitedly. Then, moving on, WALL•E felt the cockroach settling happily on his shoulder, enjoying the new, smoother ride.

WALL•E rolled past a BnL billboard, activating its holographic message as he moved. The image buzzed to life. Several loudspeakers began broadcasting the chipper voice of a human announcer, recorded centuries ago.

"Too much garbage in your face?
There's plenty of space out in space!
BnL star liners leaving each day.
We'll clean up the mess while you're away!"

WALL·E headed across a bumpy flyover, activating another ancient billboard. Through the smoggy haze, the image of a sparkling BnL star liner flashed onto the screen. Its happy passengers appeared to be enjoying all the amenities of a luxury cruise ship.

"The jewel of the BnL fleet: The *Axiom*!" the announcer's voice boomed. "Spend your five-year cruise in style. . . ." But the people had been gone from Earth far longer than five years.

"The *Axiom*!" the voice exclaimed proudly. "Putting the 'star' in 'executive star liner'."

The wind was starting to howl now. WALL·E squinted and turned on a set of tiny windscreen wipers to clean the lenses of his eyes. Looking across a bay that had dried up long ago, he saw a battered old BnL truck. WALL·E's spirits rose.

CHAPTER 2

WALL•E picked up his pace as he headed towards his truck. He scurried up and pulled a lever on the truck's side. Slowly the back began to come down, and WALL•E happily sped up the ramp and into the trailer. Home!

The wind whipped the truck as WALL•E peeled his new rubber treads from his wheels. He would put them on again in the morning before returning to work. But now it was time to relax. He removed a battered BnL cooler from his back. It was his collection box, and he was ready to begin the nightly ritual of going through the treasures he had found in the trash during the day.

But first, WALL•E went to an old television set and turned on his favourite video: *Hello, Dolly!*

He always played it when he arrived home. After watching the video for a minute, he turned back to press a button that activated the rotating racks of shelves where he neatly stored his treasures. The day had yielded some very special finds: a few old toys and utensils (all of which made WALL·E curious, since he didn't know what they were) and a lighter.

As he listened to the background music from the video, WALL·E perked up. He moved among his many treasures, stopping often in front of the fuzzy images scrolling across his television screen. The actors were singing and dancing to the song WALL·E had been humming all day. He paused, waiting for the next part. When it came, he hit the Record button on his chest and moved closer. WALL·E could see that the actors were not dancing now. They were walking together and looking into each other's eyes. Then they took each other's hands.

WALL·E tilted his head, his large eyes gazing

tenderly at the screen. He interlocked his own two robotic hands. And for a moment the lonely robot wondered what it would be like to hold someone else's hand.

Later that night, when the storm had ended, WALL•E rolled outside and turned over his collection box to clean it out. He pressed the Play button on his chest and listened to the song again. Although the little robot wasn't programmed to understand romance, it was romance that pulsed through his circuits. It was this same strange impulse that made WALL•E gaze up at the few stars visible through the polluted haze and wish for someone to share his world.

Suddenly, WALL•E's internal systems gave him a warning sign. The wind was picking up again. WALL•E checked the horizon. A massive sandstorm was approaching across the dried-up bay.

WALL•E swiftly headed back into the truck. He was familiar with the dangers of being caught in a sandstorm – air so clogged with dirt and debris that he wouldn't be able to see; whipping winds that would fill every crevice in his robotic joints with sand; and, of course, the chance of being buried. This time he was lucky: he was close to the safety of his truck.

A blinding wave of sand roared closer as WALL•E entered the truck and began to raise its door. He stopped for a moment, remembering, and then turned and made a robotic noise – like a whistle – to call for his cockroach. The door shut just as the storm hit, with both master and pet safe inside their little home.

WALL•E unwrapped a BnL sponge cake and set it on a shelf. Still moist from the preservatives that had kept it intact for centuries, the little cake made a comfy cockroach bed.

WALL•E collapsed into a box shape and backed into an empty shelf. Rocking the shelf back and forth like a cradle, he closed his eyes and shut down for the night. Outside, the full force of the storm raged across the terrain.

CHAPTER 3

"WARNING! WARNING! WARNING!" WALL•E's charge-meter light flashed at a dangerously low level the next morning.

"Mmrrr," WALL•E groaned. It was hard to wake up! Still groggy, he made his way outside and crawled up a ramp of trash to the top of his truck. Once settled, he opened his solar panels to the hazy Sun. He stretched his tiny arms and felt a surge of power run through his little cables. Finally feeling awake, he heard his solar panel chime, indicating that his electronics were fully charged for a day's work.

WALL•E happily got down from the roof and fastened his collection box to his back. He was ready to head out to work. As he rolled down the truck's ramp, suddenly – *CRUNCH!*

Horrified, WALL·E realized that he had accidentally rolled over the cockroach! WALL·E moved away and stared at his pet's flattened body.

"Ohhhh," WALL·E whined. He looked down at his pet, searching for signs of life.

POP! The bug sprang up, happy as ever, and none the worse for wear! Relieved, WALL·E let his pet hop onto his shoulder for a ride and started out again.

The day began with the usual task a WALL·E unit would expect to perform on a desolate, trash-filled planet: compacting trash. But for WALL·E, the garbage contained treasures. Thinking beyond his robotic programming, WALL·E was always looking for new things buried in the trash – things that he could add to his collections. Had there been any other robots or people on the planet, they might have thought it was a bit odd for a bot to be interested in anything other than his predetermined directive.

Today a set of car keys caught WALL•E's attention. Not knowing what they were, he went about inspecting them. He pushed the remote lock button, and somewhere deep in the trash heap a car alarm chirped. That was interesting.

Next WALL•E came across a diamond ring in a little case. He closed the case with a snap. Open. *Snap!* Close. *Snap!* The case was fun! WALL•E tossed the ring back into the trash but carefully packed up the case to take home. He also found a rubber duck, a nodding doll, and an old boot. They were definitely deserving of further attention – and possibly worthy of going into his collections.

He came across a paddle with a ball attached to it by an elastic string. When he shook it, the ball rapidly bounced against the bat. The bouncing action delighted WALL•E, until – *POP!* – the ball smacked him right between the eyes!

"Eee!" WALL•E beeped. He didn't like this

thing at all. He quickly tossed the bat aside and turned towards something else – a fire extinguisher, though WALL•E didn't know that. He simply saw something that was red and kind of heavy. WALL•E examined it until he found what he was looking for: a lever. Usually, levers activated something. WALL•E pulled it.

WHOOSH! The blast from the extinguisher propelled WALL•E into a loop-the-loop, spinning him over and over until he finally crash-landed in the trash. WALL•E moaned. He couldn't figure out what use humans had found for this shiny red object. Perhaps it had been some sort of game, but he didn't like it. Time to move on.

Digging and digging, WALL•E soon saw an old white refrigerator. He activated a welding beam between his large binocular-like eyes and cut the door down the middle. With a clang, the two pieces of the door fell off the refrigerator. WALL•E looked inside and saw a small green object in a corner. It was sprouting from a pile of dark brown soil. WALL·E gazed at it in wonder. Now, this was something really unusual. He didn't know why, but he liked it. The object had a stem with flat green ovals hanging from it. Gently, he picked it up. Making sure that it was safely cushioned in its soil, he placed it inside the old boot he'd found earlier. He tucked the object inside his box to examine later.

WALL·E sensed that the green thing was special. What he didn't know was that it was a plant.

CHAPTER 4

Thrilled with his new treasures – especially the green object – WALL•E finally returned home at the end of a long day of work. He had just reached for the lever to open his truck when a dot of red light appeared at his feet. WALL•E stopped. He stared at the dot, then slowly reached down to touch it. The dot raced away along the ground. WALL•E scurried after it. The dot led him into the vast dry bay. WALL•E was so taken by the one red dot that he didn't notice the many other dots coming at him from all sides. The little laser lights formed a circle around him.

WALL•E heard a low roar in the sky. He looked up and saw what seemed like three hot suns coming in his direction! The roar grew louder and louder. Terrified, WALL·E felt the ground shaking. Columns of fire dropped from above and surrounded him on three sides.

WALL·E furiously started to dig a hole in the ground. He jumped into it just as an intense burst of fire scorched the earth.

As suddenly as the roar had started, things quietened down. WALL·E slowly raised his head and peeked out of his hole. Something very big was looming over him. He climbed out of the hole and banged his head on a metal object.

It was the underside of some sort of spaceship!

With nowhere to hide, WALL·E made the best of what was available. He placed a small rock on his head, boxed himself up, and hoped he wouldn't be noticed. WALL·E wasn't used to visitors, so he wasn't sure what to expect. But his curiosity quickly began to get the better of him. He wanted to be able to see what was coming even while he remained hidden. Cautiously, WALL·E crept a bit closer to get a better look.

The spacecraft deposited a capsule on the ground. The capsule began to unfold, its exterior peeling away in sections. It was as if something precious were being unwrapped.

Then he saw her emerge – a sleek egg-shaped white probe-bot with gleaming blue eyes. WALL·E was breathless as he watched her hover gracefully above the ground. She was the most beautiful thing he had ever seen.

Her name was EVE.

CHAPTER 5

The spaceship began to close up. A low hum filled the air. WALL•E suddenly remembered – he was under a ship! The hum was coming from the ship's engines, which were now roaring to life. It was time to take cover again. WALL•E dug another hole in the ground and jumped into it.

When the smoke cleared, WALL•E once again raised his head. He looked up and saw EVE. She was circling over the desolate bay. As she swooped and darted like a hummingbird, she emitted a blue ray from her front panel and scanned the terrain. WALL•E scrambled out of the hole and quickly found a boulder to hide behind. He watched EVE continue to scan random objects, occasionally doing a loop in the sky. She zoomed past WALL•E's rock. Frightened yet enchanted, the rusty and dented WALL•E unit kept watching this sleek new state-of-the-art robot. This was love.

EVE gently descended to the ground, and WALL•E decided to move one rock closer to her. As he rolled forward, his treads loosened some debris – *RATTLE, RATTLE, CLUNK!*

EVE whipped around in the direction of the noise. She instantly raised and fired the blaster mounted within her arm. *KA-BLAM!* WALL•E's boulder exploded into bits. The shivering robot was unharmed but terrified.

EVE scanned the area again. All quiet, she noted, no signs of life. She moved on and wandered through WALL•E's vast avenues of trash. WALL•E rolled after her. She had just tried to blast him, but like a puppy, he continued to follow her, unable to stop.

He watched her scan a mound of tyres. Then he flinched as his cockroach decided to approach EVE from behind. Her razor-sharp sensors picked up the movement. She spun and blasted the bug with a direct hit. Unharmed, the insect simply crawled out of the smoking crater and, with his usual curiosity, continued to approach EVE.

She let the roach get closer. The little bug intrigued her, and she let him crawl up her arm. WALL•E heard her emit a series of electronic beeps. She was giggling! The roach must have tickled her.

WALL•E's spirits soared. EVE had feelings! Then, just as suddenly, he was struck by fear again as EVE's sensor turned in his direction. She locked onto him with her scanners and fired rapidly with her blaster arm.

WALL•E dodged the blasts, scooting among trash piles as EVE obliterated them one by one. With nowhere left to hide, WALL•E boxed himself up and shook uncontrollably. EVE stopped firing. Her electronics hummed, "Identify yourself." But WALL•E heard only beeps and whistles. He didn't understand what EVE was saying.

She slowly approached the shivering box. The cockroach ran down EVE's blaster arm and hopped onto his master. EVE's blue light scanned WALL•E. NEGATIVE. He was not what she was looking for. She retracted her blaster arm and glided away.

Peeking out from inside his box, WALL•E watched her, completely awestruck.

CHAPTER 6

As EVE continued her search, WALL·E followed her to an abandoned BnL store. EVE scanned the store, registering NEGATIVE, NEGATIVE, NEGATIVE.

But when she glanced back at the not-so-hidden WALL·E, the little robot panicked. Whirling awkwardly, he bumped into a rack of shopping trolleys, sending a noisy avalanche of trolleys down a flight of stairs. Unfortunately, WALL·E went tumbling and bouncing all the way down, too. Finally, the humiliating moment ended with a crash. The trolleys could move no farther, and neither could WALL·E. He was wedged between the trolleys and a pair of doors that refused to open. EVE ignored him. WALL·E began the slow process of untangling himself.

That evening, WALL•E climbed to the roof of the BnL power plant. He patiently waited, hoping to see EVE somewhere in the darkening sky. Suddenly, her blue light flashed on the horizon, and his tiny circuits skipped a beat.

WALL•E watched her come in for a landing, ready to shut down for the night. He waited, then moved towards her. Once, he accidentally tripped, but luckily the noise didn't wake her. Sure now that she was asleep, WALL•E crept closer. Carefully, he measured her dimensions with his robotic arms. Then, turning to a pile of trash, he began to weld, using the laser beam mounted between his eyes.

The next morning, EVE awoke to find a sculpture of herself made entirely of gleaming trash. Impressed, she rose and circled the egg-shaped sculpture. It had sparkling blue glass eyes, just like hers.

WALL•E watched her from behind a stack of pipes. He could see that she liked the sculpture.

Thrilled, he wanted to come out, but he hesitated . . . and the moment was gone. EVE glided away just as the pipes rolled down – *CLANK, CLANK, CLANK* – onto the happy little robot's head. Smitten as ever, he hardly noticed the extra few dents in his body.

EVE spent her day scanning the city. She scanned a car engine – NEGATIVE. She slammed the bonnet. A toilet – NEGATIVE. A space capsule – NEGATIVE. A freighter's hold – NEGATIVE.

And then something different happened: EVE got caught by the freighter's giant grey magnet! Swinging upside down, she flipped and wiggled to and fro. But no matter how hard she tried, she could not free herself from the powerful magnet.

Shhhh-lop! She freed her body, but then her arm got stuck. When she freed that one, her other arm got stuck. Frustrated by her days of fruitless searching, EVE pointed her blaster arm at the magnet and blew it up.

She watched as the flaming magnet crashed through the deck of the freighter, causing it to catch fire and topple into the next freighter. Then another freighter toppled, too, like a row of falling dominoes. It was a gigantic mess!

Oooooo! WALL·E watched as smoke from the blast enveloped EVE. She was not only beautiful but powerful, too!

Then he cocked his head and looked at her again. She seemed different from before. She slumped. It looked as if she was ready to give up.

Cautiously, WALL·E – still blinded by love – climbed onto the other side of the anchor and very slowly inched towards her. Suddenly, she turned to him and hummed, "So what's your name?"

WALL·E was so shocked that he tumbled over backwards.

EVE tried again. "Directive?" she asked. WALL·E was stunned by the sounds she was making. She was trying to communicate with him.

Even better, she didn't seem to want to use her blaster arm!

Though EVE spoke in a lovely hum, WALL•E could not understand a bit of it until he recognised the word "directive." Eager to connect with EVE, he loaded a pile of trash into his compactor and plunked down a cube for her. He struggled to speak, to let her know that this was his directive. "Di . . . rec . . . t – "

"Directive!" EVE interrupted sharply, helping him finish. His eyes grew large as he looked at her, wanting to know her purpose, too. But EVE hummed, "Classified." Her directive was a secret.

"Oh." WALL•E had hoped to learn more.

EVE scanned WALL•E's chest logo. "So what's your name?" she hummed robotically again.

Struggling to answer, WALL•E tried to form his beeping noises into the sound of his name. "WALL•E."

EVE nodded and repeated: "Waaaleeee." To the little robot, EVE's electronic voice sounded like music. He scooted a bit closer. "Waaa-lleee," EVE said again. Then she spoke her own name: "Eeeve."

"Eee-vah?" WALL·E said slowly.

EVE shook her head. "Eeeve, Eeeve."

WALL·E made the sound again: "Eee-vah!"

WALL·E heard her giggle. It was the happiest day of his life. He said it again, hoping she would giggle once more. "Eee-vah!" he said. "Ee – "

One of WALL·E's electronic warnings went off. The wind was whistling through the bay. A storm was coming – a big one. WALL·E reached for EVE's hand, but she pulled back, not understanding the danger of the situation. The sandstorm hit in a rush of swirling wind and debris. WALL·E collapsed into a box.

"WALL·E! WALL·E! WALL·E!" he heard EVE cry.

Through the blinding dust, WALL·E popped up from the safety of his box shape, reached out to EVE, and led her to shelter.

CHAPTER 7

WALL•E pulled EVE inside his truck and closed the door tight. EVE looked around, intrigued by WALL•E's many collections.

WALL•E sensed her interest and proudly began to give her a tour. First, he handed her an eggbeater. As he looked for something else to show her, EVE spun the egg-whisk faster and faster, until it whirled itself into pieces. Uh-oh. EVE quickly hid it, not wanting WALL•E to see what she had done.

But WALL•E had his mind on something else: the clear plastic wrap that had bubbles in it. Once again, EVE seemed delighted. He showed her how to pop the bubbles, then handed it to her and popped a few more bubbles encouragingly. She tried it, and then began a rapid-fire popping. In seconds, the entire sheet was deflated. This was fun!

And then WALL•E handed her his prized *Hello, Dolly!* videocassette – not expecting that she would pull the tape out of it! Emitting a high-pitched beep, WALL•E grabbed the cassette from EVE and carefully reeled the tape back inside. Terrified that it might not work, he inserted the cassette in his video player.

After an anxious moment of staring at his television, WALL•E saw his beloved characters appear on the screen, singing and dancing.

Relieved, WALL•E shuffled back-and-forth on his treads and mimicked the dancing for EVE. Extending his hand to the floor, he encouraged her to try, too.

EVE fell – *THUNK!* – to the floor and bounced back up again. WALL•E then tried a move he hoped would be less dangerous. He spun with his little shovel arms extended outwards. EVE happily imitated him – but with a massive force that quickly sent her whirling out of control! *KLANK!* EVE accidentally propelled WALL•E into a wall of shelves. As he fell to the floor, his head clanged like a bell.

EVE gasped. One of WALL•E's binocular-like eyes was hanging loose.

WALL•E calmly reassured the distraught EVE. He felt his way through a pile of spare WALL•E-unit parts. Then he popped in a spare eye and brightly turned to EVE. Good as new!

As they continued exploring WALL•E's collections, EVE amazed WALL•E by producing a flame from an old lighter. As they stared at the flame, WALL•E realized he had never been this close to EVE. He looked up at her, the flame flickering between them. In the background, his favourite song from *Hello, Dolly!* played.

WALL•E reached for EVE's hand. Maybe now he could finally hold hands with her.

EVE turned to look at him, but WALL•E

panicked and pulled his hand back, pretending to retrieve something from the floor.

Still, he wasn't about to give up. As EVE continued to stare at the television screen, WALL•E scurried off. There was one more thing that might win EVE's approval. It was the undisputed masterpiece of his many collections. He tapped her on the shoulder and held up the plant.

EVE's blue light immediately locked onto it. Her chest opened. WALL•E was shocked to see a tractor beam suddenly shoot from EVE's chest and envelop the plant. The beam had pulled the plant into a compartment in EVE's chest. Her panel doors slammed, and her system shut down altogether! Only a single green light remained pulsing on her chest.

"Eee-vah?" WALL•E said numbly. He shook her gently but got no response.

WALL•E panicked. "Eee-vah? Eee-vah!" he cried.

CHAPTER 8

The next morning, WALL•E pulled EVE up to the roof of his truck. He aimed her towards the Sun and waited. But there was no change in EVE, not a single sign that she was recharging in the sunlight.

WALL•E took EVE to different places. He held an umbrella over her during a thunderstorm, and – *BOOM!* – the umbrella was struck by lightning. So was WALL•E.

WALL•E cared for EVE as she slept. When a sandstorm appeared on the horizon, he placed a barrel over her. He held the barrel steady as the sand buried him in a tiny dune.

After the storm, WALL•E had another idea. He decided that perhaps he could jump-start her electronic heart with his own. He attached the jumper cables, closed his eyes, and hoped for the best. But EVE's state-of-the-art electronic defence system was powerful and far more advanced than WALL•E's. *BOOM!* – the electric jolt toppled WALL•E.

A bit deflated but not defeated, WALL•E made a lead out of old Christmas lights, wrapped it around EVE, and whistled for his cockroach.

Pulling gently on the lead, WALL•E went for a walk with his two companions. Then WALL•E took EVE for a boat ride on a lake of steaming sludge. Using an old street sign as an oar, he rowed her to a particularly scenic scrapyard. He set her on the bonnet of a scrapped car to watch the sunset through the polluted air.

As he observed the light being refracted through the smoggy haze, the sky turned a brilliant purple and gold. To WALL•E, the worn and smoggy world he lived in suddenly took on a rosy glow. He sighed and etched WALL•E & EVE on an old post with his laser.

Later that night, WALL•E placed EVE on the roof of his truck, the solar Christmas lights around her aglow. He set up his television in front of her so that she could watch. But no matter what WALL•E tried, there was no response.

The next day, WALL•E decided to return to work. He halfheartedly got ready, then checked on EVE one more time. Leaving her on the truck's roof with the feeble hope that the Sun's rays might awaken her, he turned away. Unenthusiastically, he called to his cockroach and set out.

At his work site, WALL•E noticed that he was just going through the motions of trash compacting. He was simply following his directive, like a normal robot. His passion for interesting items was gone. WALL•E realized he'd found the one thing in all the world that made being in it worthwhile.

WALL•E stopped and pulled out his lighter. Seeing it flicker, he sighed and remembered the good times he had shared with EVE.

A gust of wind suddenly blew out the tiny flame. WALL·E looked across the dry bay towards home. Was another sandstorm blowing in? No, it was something else: a bright glow was descending from the clouds. He heard the low rumble and instantly realized that it was the spaceship that had brought EVE. He raced towards home, terrified that the ship was coming to take her back!

"Eee-vah! Eee-vah!" WALL·E called out.

As he reached the slip road near his home, WALL·E suddenly stopped short. In the distance, the probe ship was hovering over his truck. A giant robotic arm reached out and lifted EVE into the ship's hold.

"Eee-vah! Eee-vah!" WALL·E screamed as he scrambled towards her. The cargo doors closed as the rocket engines powered up.

WALL·E rushed down a hill of rubble and up a broken flyover. Then, quickly, he stopped. He placed his cockroach on the ground and gestured to him: "Stay!" The disappointed cockroach sat down, chirping impatiently.

WALL•E careered towards the spaceship and latched onto it just as a wall of flame blasted from the engines.

Inside the ship, robotic arms fastened EVE into a slot among a long row of dormant probe-bots. EVE was the only probe-bot flashing a green light.

Outside, little WALL•E was steadily climbing the side of the ship as the final engines ignited. He clamped his small hands onto a metal support rod and closed his eyes as the rocket blasted into space. On the ground, WALL•E's cockroach dutifully stayed put as he watched his master disappear into the clouds.

CHAPTER 9

As the probe ship roared through the murky brown sky, WALL·E could feel the force of Earth's gravity on his body, pulling powerfully against the acceleration of the ship. He tightened his grip on the support rod as the ship burst through Earth's atmosphere. The engines slowed down, and WALL·E, now weightless, took in the majestic splendour of all the stars sparkling in clear space.

The probe ship passed the moon, where WALL·E saw a billboard reading BNL OUTLET COMING SOON! It stood in the lunar dust, forgotten long ago.

WALL·E blinked hard and recharged his solar panels as the ship zipped past the Sun. Travelling quickly into deep space, the ship approached

Saturn. WALL·E reached out and ran his hand through the dust and ice particles that made up one of the planet's outer rings.

Mesmerised by the view, he saw a single light growing in the distance. He recognized it from the billboards he had seen on Earth. It was a gigantic luxury-class star liner. It was the *Axiom*!

The *Axiom* was enormous – wide and tall. At the lowest level, there was a garbage depot where the ship's trash was compacted and tossed into space. Just above that stretched loading docks and service-robot corridors. The next three levels were where the passengers lived: the least expensive economy-class units in the middle of the ship; coach class on the level above, with its main concourse (which looked like a huge shopping centre); and the luxury housing units overlooking the lido deck, high above them all.

The Captain and his autopilot also had a view of the lido deck from the bridge at the top of the ship. The bridge's control panels could activate practically anything on the *Axiom* – the Captain could broadcast announcements, adjust the fake Sun that shone on the passengers (which gave them a sense of the time of day), and, of course, guide the star liner through space. One day, the Captain would look down on the lido deck and activate the holo-detector, a computer designed to confirm the presence of life on Earth. Then the great machine would rise from its platform and automatically take the ship back home.

CHAPTER 10

As it approached the star liner, WALL•E's small probe ship was swallowed inside the *Axiom*'s docking bay, where it was locked safely into place.

Still clinging to the outside of the ship, WALL•E saw the loading dock come to life. From every corner, gleaming service robots of all sizes and descriptions appeared. Their names shining on their front panels, they paused until lines appeared in front of them on the floor. Apparently, the bots carried out their directives by following these preprogrammed lines around the ship.

The probe ship's cargo doors smoothly slid open, and WALL•E saw EVE. She was still shut down; only the green light on her chest was flashing.

"Eee-vah?" WALL·E whispered as a chrome-trimmed crane-bot lifted her out of the hold and lowered her onto the huge deck below. WALL·E was careful to speak softly and remain hidden.

Immediately, a squad of robots surrounded EVE. To them, she was Probe One. A tiny mint-blue robot with a bristle-brush head was beeping orders to the rest of the robots. His name was M-O. He was a microbe obliterator with one simple directive: clean.

M-O scanned EVE. Disgusted, he computed that she was fifteen percent contaminated with dirt. He signalled his crew, who hurried along bright red lines on the floor to begin the cleanup. A vacuum-bot, a sprayer-bot, and a buffer-bot zipped along their lines to do their jobs.

WALL·E watched as the crane-bot lifted one of the bots from the probe ship and lowered it onto the deck. WALL·E suddenly had an idea. He wedged himself into another probe-bot's place, and the crane-bot picked him up next.

As M-O continued to scan the probe-bots on deck, he suddenly came across WALL•E, who was boxed up and nervously trying to blend in. M-O turned to the boxed robot and scanned him: 100% FOREIGN CONTAMINANT! A red light popped out atop M-O's head and a siren began to wail.

Poor WALL•E, having spent centuries cubing trash, was very dirty indeed. M-O instantly charged at WALL•E in a cleaning frenzy. Frightened, WALL•E pushed him away with his front panel.

M-O tried again. WALL•E rolled backwards, leaving a dirty trail on M-O's immaculate floor. M-O lunged forward and scrubbed at the track marks. Amused by his power over the cleaning-obsessed M-O, WALL•E had another idea. Just to see what might happen, he decided to stick out his tread and make another spot on the floor. M-O leaned over and scrubbed at it compulsively.

Teasing him now, WALL•E wiped one of his treads on M-O's head. M-O went crazy, trying to rid himself of the yucky stuff.

Suddenly, two steward-bots – the policing bots of the *Axiom* – emerged from a wall. Nearby, a small robot shot out of a pneumatic tube and into the docking bay. It was Gopher, the Captain's personal assistant. He quickly gave orders to the steward-bots. Then he headed towards the probe-bots. A blaring siren sounded, prompting the cleaning crew to snap to attention.

Gopher began to scan each probe-bot. He checked WALL•E and then moved on to the next robot. Realizing that something wasn't quite right, he stopped for a moment. He turned to look WALL•E over again, but the little robot was gone. Gopher continued until he finally came to EVE.

Gopher scanned EVE, and instantly, every alarm on deck began to sound. Green lights flashed everywhere. A hover transporter glided up to Gopher. He beeped and ordered the crane-bot to lift EVE into the vehicle. Gopher climbed into the driver's seat and navigated the transporter into an open lift.

"Eee-vah!" WALL•E called, hurrying after the transporter. He managed to hop inside the lift just before its doors closed.

Behind him, the other bots began to file out of the loading dock. Each robot moved strictly along its designated line. M-O discovered WALL•E's latest filthy trail. But the dirt veered away from M-O's designated line, and bots were never supposed to go off their designated lines. Not ever.

M-O looked at his departing crew, then back at the dirt that irresistibly called to him. He closed his eyes and did something no service robot aboard the *Axiom* had ever done: he jumped off his designated line. Somehow, WALL•E had had a strong effect on the industrious cleaner-bot.

Cringing, M-O slowly opened his eyes. He looked around cautiously. No alarms. No whistles. Nothing had happened! That wasn't so hard, he decided, and cheerily began following WALL•E's tracks, scrubbing as he went. He was determined to find and clean this bot.

CHAPTER 11

Inside the transporter, as Gopher patiently waited at the wheel, WALL•E could feel the lift rising. An instant later, the lift doors opened. WALL•E got his first look at the ship's robot passageway, which was located above the docking bay. Robots were zipping by at lightning speed.

Gopher smoothly turned into the traffic as WALL•E tried – and failed – to merge. He put one tread into the traffic and yanked it back, causing a pile-up of mangled robots. Whoops! He heard multiple beeps of objection from the busy bots.

WALL•E was too frightened to move, but the transporter carrying EVE was getting farther and farther away. Bravely, he decided to box up and try again. Disregarding all robot traffic rules and every designated line, WALL•E rolled towards EVE.

Weaving in and out of traffic, he spotted EVE on her transporter up ahead. It was gliding towards an off-ramp. WALL•E chased the transporter and suddenly emerged onto the deck above. Blinking, he saw the bright lights of the *Axiom*'s economy-class courtyard.

WALL•E noticed that the courtyard was surrounded by hundreds of guest rooms. Passengers filled the giant courtyard, reclining in chairs that hovered just above the floor. WALL•E looked at their faces. Humans had changed over the centuries. They didn't look like the photos in the old magazines and newspapers that littered Earth's surface. These humans were very large and very soft. Their legs had turned flabby from lack of exercise, and their necks didn't seem to exist at all.

WALL•E waved happily even though no one waved back. Moving forward, WALL•E tilted his head and saw the holographic screens that all the reclining humans had in front of their faces. He noticed that what the humans lacked in leg strength, they more than made up for in powerful high-tech devices that provided them with information, fed them, and even moved them. The humans seemed bored and without purpose. Their world was completely digital. No one had any motivation to do anything. Bots served the humans' every need.

Still, WALL•E kept waving at them. He had not seen a human being in centuries!

Two passengers, John and Buddy, drifted by, boxed into their chairs with speakers on either side of their heads and holographic screens in front of their faces. They could easily have spoken to each other directly . . . if they had had the motivation and ability to turn their heads and push aside the electronics surrounding them. Instead, they were isolated in the midst of a crowd of humanity, not even caring or knowing that they were right next to each other. WALL•E tried to follow and understand what they were saying.

"So what do you wanna do?" "I don't know. What do you wanna do?"

WALL•E saw Buddy's screen flash a virtual amusement park. "Let's ride the roller coaster again," Buddy said.

"Nah," John responded. "I've already ridden that a thousand times."

"Well, then what do you want to do?" Buddy asked.

"I don't know."

WALL•E left the arguing humans behind as he pursued the transporter into a tunnel crowded with robots and more humans in hover chairs. For a moment, the screens connecting the humans flickered. The humans began to panic. They stopped talking and typed words like "Oh no, you're breaking up!" and "I can't hear you! I'm in a tunnel."

When the human passengers were disengaged from their electronics, it was frightening for them. But they quickly calmed down when the tunnel emptied into the star liner's main concourse. "You're back! I can hear you now!" the relieved passengers shouted. Their hover chairs glided across the main concourse.

The concourse was a city-sized mall. On the upper level surrounding the mall, WALL•E saw endless rows of guest suites.

He looked up, trying to take in his new surroundings. Everything was available to meet all the passengers' needs and desires – instant foods in the form of shakes, robots to give them massages and haircuts – but there was nothing that really drew the humans away from the holo-screens in front of them.

An announcer's voice suddenly filled the air. WALL•E jumped. "Happy *Axiom* Day!" the voice said, cheerfully booming across the deck. "Your day is very important to us! If you're not happy, you're not consuming!"

WALL•E didn't understand. He just wanted to find EVE.

CHAPTER 12

WALL·E moved forward . . . and wandered across one of the lines on the floor. This broke the rules. He accidentally bumped into one of the passengers. Then WALL·E bumped into John, knocking him off his chair.

"Help!" John screamed, panicking. He didn't know what to do without his hover chair! He couldn't move! (Well, he could wriggle and scream, but he couldn't do much more than that.) The reclining passengers continued to glide by, not even noticing him. WALL·E lifted the helpless, overweight man into his chair. John stared at the strange bot. He settled into the cocoon of his artificial environment, but he would not forget the little robot who had just rescued him.

WALL•E saw Gopher driving the transporter that held EVE onto a monorail packed with passengers. WALL•E manoeuvred across the crowded floor, barely catching the monorail's last car.

WALL•E had to make his way forward through the cars to get to EVE. The monorail kept moving forward, too. As it zipped past dozens of themed restaurants in the food court, the smells of tacos and teriyaki wafted through the air. Service-bots shoved samples at the passengers.

"Mmmm, time for lunch!" the ship's announcer said. Instantly, large quantities of each speciality were served on every armrest.

The monorail passed a beauty salon where passengers were being polished and pampered. WALL•E heard the ship's announcer croon, "Feel beautiful!"

When the monorail rolled through the fashion district, everyone's screen suddenly flashed "Attention, *Axiom* shoppers! Try blue. It's the new red!" Within moments, the passengers' jumpsuits turned from red to bright blue. WALL•E looked at his own rusted exterior. It stayed its usual dirty brown.

WALL•E held on to the back of a seat as the monorail sped through a long tunnel. He was slowly making his way towards EVE.

But a human passenger named Mary blocked the way. She was chattering at her screen.

"Date? Don't get me started!" she said, annoyed. "Every holo-date I've been on has been a virtual disaster! If I could just meet someone who wasn't so superficial . . ."

WALL•E twisted and turned, trying to get around Mary, but she didn't seem to notice him.

"Him?" she said, completely unaware of WALL•E. "If he was any more into himself, you wouldn't be able to see his head."

Desperate to get to EVE, WALL•E pulled himself up onto Mary's headrest and speakers. They broke off. *Blink!* Mary's holographic screen shorted out.

Mary was stunned. Her tiny but complex electronic system was wiped out. She looked from side to side, forced to take in the world around her. Astounded, she looked down and saw her own feet! Wiggling her toes, she adjusted her seat to an upright position to get a better view.

When Mary moved, WALL•E zoomed past her. But he didn't realize what he had done for her. From now on, she would experience life instead of having it served to her.

The monorail doors slid open and a voice announced their arrival on the lido deck.

A first-class tropical paradise, the lido deck was surrounded by dazzling white high-rise apartments and a plaza filled with sparkling pools.

Passengers reclining in their hover chairs followed the red lines onto the luxurious deck as Mary, the only passenger who was actually seeing it, rose to her little feet, stumbled forward, and exclaimed, "I didn't know we had a pool!"

CHAPTER 13

The monorail glided across the lido deck, finally stopping at the entrance to the ship's bridge. Gopher drove the transporter into the bridge's enormous lobby, where it stopped and beeped at the desk of a lonely typing-bot. A gate was lowered and the transporter whooshed through.

WALL·E emerged onto the bridge and hid in the shadows of a huge circular room. The bridge was where the Captain and Auto, the *Axiom*'s autopilot and steering wheel, controlled the ship.

Auto seemed to dominate the room. With a large eye in the centre of his wheel, he could view both the lido deck and deep space just outside the window. He had a long mechanical tentacle that he used as a hand to help him push buttons or lift things, and even lift objects periodically.

Gopher saluted Auto and presented EVE for inspection. WALL•E watched as Auto scanned EVE and began computing rapidly until a code blinked on his screen. Auto and Gopher exchanged several beeps and nodded.

WALL•E felt the floor beneath him move. Stifling a shriek, he realized – too late – that he was standing on a trapdoor. It opened to the Captain's quarters one floor below . . . which was exactly where WALL•E landed when he fell.

Auto, not noticing WALL•E, reached down through the hole right behind him and activated the Captain's alarm clock. WALL•E boxed up in the dark room and hid.

"Captain," Auto said to a snoring body in a bed, "you are needed on the bridge." Auto then retreated to the bridge.

With no one else there but the sleeping Captain, WALL•E glanced around the dimly lit room. The walls were covered with portraits of former captains, their years of service listed beneath their names. The date under the first portrait was 2105. That was seven centuries ago, when the *Axiom* had been launched from Earth for its five-year cruise. It was now 695 years behind schedule for its return.

The captains had changed over time, growing larger and flabbier. Like the humans on the ship, the captains had declined, each one visibly less spirited than his or her predecessors.

The current captain reached out to silence his alarm and accidentally pushed a button on WALL•E's chest instead. WALL•E cringed. The music of *Hello, Dolly!* blasted from his speaker.

The Captain flopped around in his bed, flustered. "All hands on deck!" he muttered. "What? Who? Who's there?" he asked, only half awake.

Luckily for WALL•E, a group of prep-bots filed into the room . . . and he found the Off button for the music. A beautician-bot, a massage-bot, and a wardrobe-bot surrounded the Captain's bed, which converted into a chair as the robots obediently brushed, massaged, and dressed the groggy human.

WALL•E tried to blend in by rubbing the Captain's feet. He accidentally tickled the Captain, making him giggle. Fortunately, WALL•E remained unnoticed, and he decided it was best to simply hide under the Captain's chair.

"Oh, you look gorgeous!" the beautician-bot said. The Captain nodded as his hover chair glided up towards the bridge. WALL•E clung to the underside of the Captain's chair. The hover chair would take him back to the bridge – and EVE.

CHAPTER 14

On the ship's bridge, Auto stood to attention, awaiting the arrival of the Captain. With a whir from his hover chair, the Captain finally entered the bridge. A coffee-bot rose from the console as WALL·E scooted out of sight.

"Sir," Auto said, unblinking.

"Coffee," the Captain demanded, heading for the large console.

Auto tried again. "Sir, the annual–"

The Captain held his hand up in Auto's direction. Trying to manoeuvre his large body, he adjusted his chair and was almost able to reach the coffee cup. "Protocol, Auto. First things first," he said, finally grabbing the cup and taking a sip.

The Captain was in no hurry. There was no

need for anyone to navigate the huge star liner. The *Axiom* had been in a holding pattern around Earth's galaxy for more than seven hundred years. At this stage, Auto controlled the ship far more than the Captain did.

The Captain's chair slowly followed a red line around the console. Panels lit up as he passed. "Mechanical systems?" the bored Captain asked the ship's computer.

"Unchanged," the computer answered.

"Reactor core temperature? Passenger count? Regenerative foodstuffs? Jacuzzi temperature? Waste flow? Laundry-service volume? Buffet menu?"

"Unchanged, unchanged, unchanged," the computer responded. The Captain's work day was over. He was about to order up the buffet when he glanced at the time. He flashed Auto a look. It was past noon!

"Sir, the annual recon–" Auto started. Auto wanted to tell the Captain about EVE.

"Twelve-thirty? Auto, you let me sleep in again!" the Captain complained.

"Sir – " Auto began. But the Captain snapped like a slingshot across to the bridge's lido deck side, his voice booming out over the passengers.

"The morning announcements," the Captain said. He turned a dial on the console and cranked the Sun from midday back to sunrise. He smiled smugly. Now he hadn't overslept. Auto rolled his huge eye.

On the lido deck, passengers' lunch drinks were automatically switched to breakfast drinks, but no one seemed to care.

The Captain now appeared on every passenger's screen. A section of the fake sky became a large video display broadcasting his image.

"Good morning, ladies and gentlemen," he said in the competent voice of an experienced pilot. "Welcome to day 255,600 of the *Axiom*'s five-year cruise." It was the seven hundredth anniversary of the *Axiom*'s launch into space!

The Captain cheerfully announced that each passenger would receive a free cupcake to celebrate the occasion.

The Captain paused, noticing a flashing button on the console. "Hey? Hey, Auto, what is that flashing button? Auto?" he said, his microphone still on. "What the – ?" Luckily, the microphone finally turned off.

Inside the bridge, the Captain had finally noticed EVE. Auto was reactivating her.

From under the console, WALL•E saw EVE return to life! Her white egglike shell was glowing again, and her soft blue eyes slowly opened.

"Eee-vah!" he said joyfully. WALL•E had caught up with EVE at last, and she was awake – alive! – again. Of course, he wasn't sure what he would do next. But at least he was with his true love!

CHAPTER 15

All business-like, EVE saluted the Captain. She was fully prepared to complete her directive – the secret directive she had refused to tell WALL·E about back on Earth.

The Captain stared at her. He noticed the green light flashing on her chest. It matched the green light flashing on his console. Not knowing what any of it meant, the Captain pushed the console button, just to see what would happen. The room suddenly went dark, and a holographic screen displaying the image of BnL's CEO appeared.

"Greetings and congratulations, Captain!" the CEO declared brightly. "If you're seeing this, that means your Extraterrestrial Vegetation Evaluator, or 'EVE' probe, has returned from Earth with a confirmed specimen of ongoing photosynthesis.

That's right," he added. "It means it's time to go back home!"

"Home?" the Captain said blankly to Auto. "Does he mean *home* home?"

Auto turned slightly, hardly acknowledging the question, as the CEO told them, "Now that Earth has been restored to a life-sustaining status, by golly, we can begin *Operation: Recolonise*!" An ancient, dusty manual slid out of the console. The Captain took it and blew the dust from its cover as the CEO continued: "Simply follow this manual's instructions to place the plant in your ship's holo-detector, and the *Axiom* will immediately navigate your return to Earth. It's that easy!"

The Captain looked at the manual again. The ship's holo-detector was out on the lido deck. If he just had to activate the holo-detector and put the plant in it, why bother with the manual, especially since it didn't seem to be working?

He couldn't find a button on it anywhere.

The CEO's message continued: "Now, due to the effects of microgravity, you and your passengers may have suffered some slight bone loss. But I'm sure a few laps around your ship's jogging track will get you back in shape in no time."

The overweight Captain looked confused. "We have a jogging track?" he asked Auto.

"Seriously," the CEO's recorded voice said, brimming with confidence. "If you have any further questions, just consult your operation manual." He flashed a big white BnL smile and said, "See you back home, real soon!"

The transmission ended. The stunned Captain held up the manual. He paused for a moment, not knowing what to do with it. Finally, he gave a command to it: "Operate!" Nothing happened.

Auto took the manual, opened it, and returned it to the Captain.

"Oh . . . will you look at that!" the Captain said. It had been a long time since he had read more than a simple line or two on a video screen. It had been even longer since any human had picked up a book and actually read it. "Oooh, that's a lot of words!"

As the Captain and Auto tried to read the manual, WALL•E couldn't resist moving closer to EVE. He tapped her on the shoulder. "WALL•E!" she exclaimed.

He gave her a tiny wave. But EVE worried that he might interfere with her directive, so she beeped and gestured for him to hide and stay quiet.

WALL•E just stared, thinking every sound and movement she made was simply amazing. "Eee-vah!" he sighed.

Auto and the Captain turned their attention back to EVE. "Well, let's open her up," the Captain said, humming a tune from *Hello, Dolly!* He didn't realize that he was remembering the music he had awakened to, the music that had come from WALL•E. He liked that song.

"Do you know what that song is?" he asked Auto. "It's been running through my head all morning."

EVE stood at attention, ready to present the plant that would complete her directive and start the process of sending the *Axiom* back to Earth.

But when she opened her storage compartment, it was empty. The plant was gone!

The Captain looked at Auto. "Where's the . . . thingie?"

"Plant," Auto replied.

"Plant. Right. Right," the Captain said. "Where is it?" He looked at the manual. "Maybe we missed a step," he said, thumbing through the pages. "Show me how you change the text again."

As Auto tried to help the Captain, EVE turned to WALL•E. "Plant! WALL•E!" she said impatiently. She thought he had taken the plant.

WALL•E looked back at her, wide-eyed.

"WALL•E!" she said sternly. She scanned his chest and found nothing. She picked him up and scanned the floor. Nothing was underneath. "Plant!" EVE demanded.

Confused and concerned, WALL·E scurried around, searching for the plant.

"Why don't you scan her, just to be sure?" the Captain said to Auto.

Auto reported a negative. "Contains no specimen," he told the Captain, and added, "Probe memory is faulty."

The Captain's excitement turned to disappointment. "So, then, we're not going to Earth?" he asked the unblinking eye.

"Negative," Auto replied.

The Captain nodded. "The probe must be defective. Send her to the repair ward."

Gopher immediately appeared from a pneumatic tube. He enveloped EVE in the energy bands used to restrain defective robots, then lifted her back into the transport.

"And have them run diagnostics. Make sure she is not malfunctioning," the Captain continued.

As EVE was carted off, the Captain finally saw WALL•E alone on the floor. The Captain stared at him for a moment. WALL•E waved innocently and shook the Captain's hand happily. "And fix that robot as well," the Captain ordered, as he wiped his hand, soiled by WALL•E's handshake. "Have it hosed down, or something. It's filthy."

CHAPTER 16

As WALL·E and EVE were placed back in the transport, the Captain remained on the bridge, thumbing through the manual. "'. . . And the internal gyroscope will level out," he read, intrigued by the real workings of space travel.

He looked at his hand and noticed the filthy reminder of WALL·E's handshake. Reaching to clean it off, he paused, then took a sample and placed it on the console. Seconds later, the dirt was suspended in a beam of light.

The holo-screen showed pictures of dirt, and a computer voice announced, "Analysis: soil, dirt, or earth."

The Captain was curious. His eyes drifted towards a holographic globe on a shelf. "Define 'earth'," he told the ship's computer.

"Earth," it responded, as the beauty of forests and rolling green hills appeared on the screen. "The surface of the world as distinct from the sky or sea."

"Define 'sea'," the Captain said, fascinated.

Great foaming blue waves suddenly appeared on his screen. The Captain was spellbound. In his relentless pursuit of EVE and true love, WALL•E was slowly affecting those around him. Even the Captain was showing interest in something. Like Mary, he was noticing a whole new world. He was enjoying being engaged in something beyond a digital experience.

At that same moment, WALL•E and EVE were being shuttled through the transport tunnel. WALL•E tried to catch EVE's eye, but she refused to look at him.

WALL•E and EVE were taken into the chaos of the ship's huge repair ward. Malfunctioning robots, confined by energy bands, chatted noisily and behaved wildly. Not realizing that they were defective, the bots tried to continue with their directives, making quite a scene. WALL•E spotted an over-anxious massage-bot tearing a crash-test dummy to bits. In a corner, a mad defibrillator-bot was wildly waving his paddles, zapping at anything within his reach.

An orderly locked a red "defect" device onto EVE's head. These non-removable devices made it difficult for the bots to escape the repair ward. The orderlies started towards WALL•E with one of the devices, but he dodged them and escaped before they could tag him. His goal was to get away and save EVE.

And then . . . he was snatched by a defective beautician-bot, who slapped make-up onto his face. She held a mirror up and shouted, "You look gorgeous!"

Now thoroughly confused, WALL•E finally got caught in the robotic arms of one of the orderlies. The robot secured him to a spot along the wall.

WALL•E was locked down between a paint-bot, who was spraying paint everywhere, and a defective vacuum-bot, who was sneezing dust into WALL•E's face. It was not the best place to be locked down.

Rotating his head to peer past his two new companions, WALL•E watched the orderlies take EVE to be inspected. He could see her outline through the frosted glass of the diagnostic room.

WALL•E heard a defective bot howling somewhere in the repair ward. He was sure it was EVE. And he was sure they were hurting her!

A surge of energy rushed through WALL•E's circuits. Desperate to save her, he used the laser beam between his eyes to cut himself free. He fell to the ground, landing on his Play button. The same *Hello, Dolly!* song that had awakened the Captain earlier now blared across the repair ward. Every reject-bot froze. They all turned towards WALL•E. Stunned, they watched him crash through the glass doors and grab EVE's blaster arm, which the technician-bots had just removed.

WALL•E was trembling, but the message to the orderlies was clear: *Let her go, or else!*

The orderlies sprang at WALL•E, and in a moment of bumbling panic, he fired EVE's blaster. Fortunately, he was holding the blaster backwards. The shot went wild, shattering the repair ward's control panel to smoking bits.

The blue energy bands around the reject-bots instantly disappeared. The trembling rejects were released! They stared for a moment and then cheered wildly.

EVE glared at WALL•E. He realized she had not been hurt after all. But now she certainly was angry.

"WALL•E!" she said sternly as a mob of excited rejects raced towards him. They lifted WALL•E onto their shoulders and carried their hero out of the ward. EVE followed, astonished, as sirens began to wail throughout the ship.

The escaping bots stampeded through the

halls. Umbrella-bots randomly opened and closed, and the paint-bot hurled paint in every direction. WALL•E helplessly bounced on top of the heap, still holding EVE's blaster arm.

A line of steward-bots appeared, blocking the reject-bots.

"Halt!" a steward barked.

WALL•E cowered. A small robot came forward and pushed his hero WALL•E closer to the stewards.

The reject-bots, anxiously awaiting the stewards' next move, suddenly saw EVE flying overhead. She swooped down, snatched her blaster arm, and yelled, "WALL•E!"

The steward-bots snapped their photo, and an image of WALL•E and EVE waving her dangerous blaster arm flashed across every screen in the *Axiom*.

"Caution!" the ship's computer announced. "Rogue robots! Rogue robots!"

Now they were really in trouble. WALL•E and

EVE looked like criminals!

The stewards were preparing to lock WALL•E in a suspension beam when EVE snatched him up by his arm. She carried him high above their heads.

The reject-bots held back the steward-bots as EVE flew WALL•E through the crowded halls. She heard service robots shriek when they identified WALL•E and EVE as the blaster-arm-toting twosome on their screens. EVE looked for a place to hide.

She pushed WALL•E into a lift. As it descended, their WANTED! image appeared on the lift's screen. "Caution! Rogue robots!" blared on its speakers.

"Eee-vah!" WALL•E pointed excitedly to the picture of the two of them on the screen. He thought they looked a bit like the romantic couple in his favourite movie. But EVE realized that they looked like fugitives. She drew her arm back and blasted the screen to pieces.

CHAPTER 17

WALL•E and EVE quietly entered the dark control room of the ship's emergency escape centre. EVE found her way to the console that controlled the escape pods. She began tapping commands into the keyboard.

WALL•E glanced down at EVE's hand. He interlocked his own hands and thought that perhaps this was the right moment to take hers. "Eee-vah?" he said softly.

Before he could take her hand, the control console's lights blinked on and an escape pod appeared at the end of the room. Its hatch slowly tilted open.

EVE turned to WALL•E. "Earth," she said, pointing to an overhead screen. The screen displayed the coordinates of WALL•E's smoggy home planet.

She gestured for WALL•E to enter the pod, and the little robot rolled in. He looked back happily and patted the seat next to him. He was waiting for EVE to join him. But EVE wasn't moving. WALL•E gestured again for her to come, but she shook her head. She pointed to her chest and made her plant symbol glow.

"Directive," she said. She would stay behind to complete her directive.

As soon as WALL•E realized she wasn't going with him, he raced out of the pod and boxed up.

EVE sighed. She wanted WALL•E to go home and be safe. Then she could complete her directive without all the trouble he was causing her. She picked him up and carried him back into the pod. WALL•E raced out and tried to hide behind the console.

"WALL•E," EVE said, staring impatiently at the love-struck robot.

The chime of the lift interrupted their standoff. Someone was coming!

EVE quickly shut down the control panel and retreated into the shadows with WALL·E. They heard something motor into the room, but it was too dark to see what it was.

An arm rose up to the console, and a robotic hand worked the keyboard. The lights blinked back on. In the glow, WALL·E and EVE saw . . . Gopher. The two bots exchanged a confused glance as Gopher removed something from his chest panel and placed it in the pod.

It was the plant! Shocked, EVE realized that Gopher had been working against her all along. He must have taken the plant from her while she was shut down.

WALL·E gazed at EVE. Now there was proof that he hadn't taken the plant from her! EVE acknowledged this with a sheepish shrug. She looked up to see Gopher returning to the console. He tapped another series of buttons.

When she turned back to WALL•E, he was gone. "WALL•E?" she whispered. He was inside the pod, trying to retrieve the plant for her.

"WALL•E!" she whispered again, calling him back. But just then, Gopher hit the launch button. *Whoosh!* The escape pod was instantly jettisoned into space. EVE watched as the plant – and WALL•E – slipped away from her.

CHAPTER 18

As Gopher exited the room, EVE rushed to an air lock. She squeezed herself in and, with the push of a button, hurled herself into space.

Inside the escape pod, a terrified WALL•E was plastered against the rear wall. When the computer reported that the pod had reached cruising speed, WALL•E and the plant dropped to the floor.

"You may now turn on all electrical devices," the computer said.

WALL•E tried to get his bearings. He looked out the hatch and saw the *Axiom* getting smaller and smaller in the distance.

He made his way to the pilot's seat and pulled back hard on the lever. Nothing happened.

Frantically, he pushed all the buttons on the console at the same time.

Lights flashed. Oxygen masks dropped from the ceiling. The windscreen wipers activated, and missiles deployed from the sides of the ship.

WALL•E kept pushing buttons. Then he hit the wrong one – the self-destruct button. "Pod will self-destruct in ten seconds," the computer said calmly. "You are now free to move about the cabin. Ten, nine, eight . . ."

WALL•E panicked. Desperately looking around for an escape, he saw a fire extinguisher and an emergency exit lever on the hatch. Hoping for the best, he grabbed the fire extinguisher and yanked the lever hard. Instantly, he was sucked into space as the pod exploded in a ball of fire beneath him.

EVE saw the escape pod blow up in the distance.

"WALL•E," she moaned, stunned. She had only meant to send the little robot home, not disintegrate him!

Suddenly, WALL•E whooshed by her. He was alive! Propelled by the fire extinguisher, he was heading right back towards the *Axiom*.

EVE turned and caught up to him.

Proudly, WALL•E opened his chest compartment and showed EVE the plant. He had saved it! EVE was delighted. She leaned towards WALL•E and a spark of energy – a robot kiss – passed between their heads.

Soon they were flying, side by side, making figure eights in perfect unison.

Inside the ship, Mary was staring out the window. She saw WALL•E and EVE dancing among the silver-white stars. "Oooh!" the human said excitedly.

Just then, John's hover chair drifted by. Mary reached out and turned off the electronics on John's armrest. He blinked and looked around.

"Hey!" Mary shouted at him. "Hey, look!"

She pointed to the window. "Look at that!" she yelled, startling John.

"Wha – !" He looked all around him. "Huh?"

Confused without his electronics, John glanced at Mary, and then out the ship's window, which displayed a glorious view of the galaxy. Like Mary, he immediately saw WALL·E and EVE gliding through space, as if they were dancing on the stars.

"Oooh!" John exclaimed in awe. He recognized that little bot.

Both Mary and John drew closer to the window to watch. After the moment had passed, John reached down to his armrest to turn his electronics back on. But Mary's hand was still there. The two hands touched. John turned to Mary, and their eyes actually met.

"Hi," John said, and smiled.

"Hi," Mary answered, smiling, too.

CHAPTER 19

Up on the ship's bridge, Auto lazily watched the lido deck's sky turn from day to evening. Just below him, in the Captain's quarters, a computer was flashing images to the Captain one after the other.

"Define 'hoedown'!" the Captain told the computer.

The computer responded, "Hoedown: a special gathering at which lively forms of dancing would take place."

The Captain slapped his knee, enjoying every bit of Earth information he could get his chubby hands on.

The ceiling portal suddenly opened and Auto descended to face the Captain. The Captain looked up.

"Auto!" he exclaimed. "Earth is amazing!" He highlighted images on his computer as he spoke. "These are called farms!" Auto turned a bored eye to the screen as the Captain showed him fields of wheat and orchards of apples. "Humans would put seeds in the ground, pour water on them, and they would grow food, like pizza!"

Auto shut the screen. "Goodnight, Captain," he said, rising back to the bridge. The lights in the Captain's quarters went dark. Auto was telling the Captain that it was time to go to bed.

"Pssst," the Captain whispered to his computer. He was like a child who wanted to stay up to play. Only, in this case, the Captain wanted to know more about Earth. "Define 'dancing'."

"Dancing," the computer began. At that moment, just outside the Captain's window, WALL·E and EVE spiralled around each other. "A series of movements involving two partners, where speed and rhythm match harmoniously with music."

Indeed, WALL·E and EVE were dancing. And, in a way, the Captain was dancing, too – at least in his mind.

Outside the *Axiom,* WALL·E's fire extinguisher spurted out its last bit of foam. He floated freely for a moment; then EVE took him in her arms to return him to the ship. To WALL·E, this was a dream come true.

Back inside the *Axiom,* EVE slowly led WALL·E down the corridors, trying to get to the Captain. A group of stewards passed by. The computer warned, "Caution! Rogue robots!" EVE pulled WALL·E aside to hide.

How could EVE get to the bridge to deliver the plant to the Captain?

CHAPTER 20

A towel trolley – with EVE and WALL·E hiding behind it – slowly moved across the lido deck as the ship's announcer said, "Attention, passengers. The lido deck is now closing." Beach umbrellas suspended over hover chairs snapped shut, and the last few passengers glided out of the pool area. They were all dressed in blue except for the two wearing red in the pool.

"Hey now, stop that!" John said, laughing as Mary splashed at him.

"Make me," she answered playfully.

"Oh! Okay." John giggled and splashed her back.

A lifeguard-bot moved down from his tower. "No splashing! No diving!"

"Ahh! Switch off!" John yelled back, splashing the annoying robot. The lifeguard-bot short-circuited and toppled over, knocking a passenger into the pool.

"Whoa!" the man yelled as he fell into the water.

"Hang on!" Mary shouted as she and John each grabbed one of the man's arms. "We've got you!" Together they managed to lift the man out of the pool and back into his chair.

The man didn't know what to say. He, too, was unused to being without his electronic devices. He was actually looking at other human beings face to face, not over some holo-screen.

"Uh . . . thank . . . you?" he tried.

"You're . . . uh . . . welcome," John said, smiling.

The towel trolley rolled by with WALL·E and EVE silently and carefully pushing it forward as it hid them from view. They could look up and see the Captain's quarters and the bridge. They were close now.

WALL•E peeked out and saw a line of stewards filling the lobby that led to the bridge. He quickly reversed the towel trolley into the shadows. EVE scanned the area, searching for another way up to the bridge.

The trash chute! EVE realized that the chute went straight up to the bridge! She raised her hand, motioning to WALL•E to stay. He shook his head in protest. But EVE looked at him and said, "Waaaleeee," just as she had done when they first met. WALL•E tilted his head and sighed. Before he knew it, he found himself watching EVE zoom past the guards at superfast speed – and right up the chute.

CHAPTER 21

Inside the Captain's quarters, a chubby hand moved a toy starship towards a holographic globe. "Prepare for landing," the Captain said, inching the small model of the *Axiom* closer to the globe.

"We're here, everybody!" he announced to his pretend passengers. He walked his fingers over the globe and said in a high voice, "Yay, Captain! It's so beautiful!"

"No, it's nothing," he said, lowering his voice again. "I was pleased to do it. It's all about you people!"

A strange rattling interrupted his make-believe landing. The Captain turned away from the globe to see EVE rising from the trash chute.

EVE hovered in front of him, and to his complete surprise, she opened her panel doors.

"The plant!" the Captain exclaimed. "How did you ever find it?"

EVE floated towards him and saluted. She presented him with the plant. He gazed at it in absolute wonder. "We can go home now!" he gasped. He looked at the holographic globe. "What's it like now?" he asked EVE anxiously. "No, no, don't tell me," he said as he activated her memory chip, causing images from her mission to Earth to flash onto his screen.

The Captain squinted as the screen jumped from one scene to another. He watched EVE's journey through her eyes – all the things she had seen and recorded during her time on Earth.

But soon the Captain's happy anticipation evaporated. His brow furrowed as he saw images of Earth's terrible condition. These pictures were nothing like the ones he'd seen earlier on his computer. He began to worry. Earth was clearly too polluted. He couldn't guide his ship home to that mess. People would not be able to live there.

He looked down at the plant. A single leaf dropped. But wait – the Captain knew what to do. He had learned this from the computer. He would water the plant.

And as he turned to do so, he heard WALL•E's favourite song playing. EVE had recorded *Hello, Dolly!* when WALL•E had shown the video to her back on Earth.

"Hey, I remember that song!" the Captain said. And somehow it inspired him.

He looked at the plant. If this little guy could grow on Earth, then his passengers could grow and thrive there, too. By golly, they could even help clean up the planet and get rid of the pollution!

EVE continued to watch as her recording device kept playing back *Hello, Dolly!* She saw how WALL•E's favourite characters intertwined their hands. She looked down at her own hands and interlocked them. Suddenly, she understood what WALL•E had been trying to do. He had wanted to hold hands . . . just like the romantic couple in his movie.

Then EVE found herself watching images of the time on Earth when she had been dormant. She saw things she hadn't known about until now – images of WALL•E caring for her as she slept; WALL•E shielding her from the rain with his umbrella; WALL•E buried in a sandstorm, trying to protect her; WALL•E keeping watch day and night while she was shut down. She even saw him trying to jump-start her heart with his own.

"WALL•E," EVE said to herself, touched by the robot's selfless devotion. Finally, she realized that WALL•E loved her!

CHAPTER 22

Pacing back and forth outside the trash chute, WALL•E suffered through several changes of mind on how to take EVE's hand: upside down, sideways, from the left, or from the right.

WALL•E became more and more impatient. At last, he looked around for a disguise and spotted the towel trolley. Covering himself in towels, he made his way to the trash chute's opening. Climbing inside, he began to crawl up the chute, using slow, crablike movements.

Meanwhile, in the Captain's quarters, EVE continued to watch images of WALL•E from her video recordings of Earth. She saw him etch their names in a heart. "WALL•E," she sighed.

The Captain was there, too. He turned to Auto,

holding the prized plant. "Auto," he said, "Probe One found the plant! Fire up the holo-detector!"

"Not necessary, Captain," Auto replied calmly. "You may give it to me."

The Captain held up a chubby finger. "You know what? I should do it myself!"

Auto shot over and blocked the Captain.

"Sir," Auto said sternly. "I insist that you give me the plant."

The Captain was shocked – and starting to get angry. Auto reported to him!

"Get out of my way," the Captain said firmly, trying to move past Auto.

"Sir, we cannot go home."

"What are you talking about, Auto? Why not?"

"That is classified," Auto said, leaning over the Captain. "Give me the plant!"

The Captain waved the plant around, out of Auto's reach. "What do you mean, 'classified'? You don't keep secrets from the Captain!"

"Give me the plant," Auto demanded.

"Tell me what's classified," the Captain snapped. "Tell me, Auto. That's an order!"

Auto finally punched a series of buttons with his robotic tentacle. A BnL message appeared on-screen. It was labelled TOP SECRET: FOR AUTOPILOT EYE ONLY.

The Captain watched as the face of BnL's leader appeared. Via the fuzzy old recording, the leader told the autopilots of all BnL star liners to take control of the ships and never return to Earth, as life there was "unsustainable."

"'Unsustainable?" The Captain scoffed. He turned his gaze from the screen to the plant in his lap. For the first time, he had seen the truth: there was no great plan to return to Earth. His company and his leader had given up on him, his ship, and his passengers. The Captain's face grew red. He was holding living proof – the plant – that life was indeed sustainable on Earth. Now he was downright angry.

CHAPTER 23

Auto held out one of his tentacled handles towards the Captain. "Now the plant."

"No!" the Captain shouted, refusing to give the plant to his autopilot. "This doesn't change anything, Auto! We have to go back!"

Auto had never expected this captain to defy him. But the Captain had finally come to the conclusion that if the little plant had grown and survived on Earth, so could the people on the *Axiom*.

"Sir," Auto answered, "orders are: do not return to Earth."

"Because he thought nothing could survive there anymore," the Captain argued. "But that was hundreds of years ago! Now look at the plant – green and growing! It's living proof!"

"Irrelevant, Captain." Auto was sticking to his directive.

"What?" the Captain said, raising his voice. "No! It's completely relevant! Out there is our home. *Home*, Auto! And it's in trouble. I can't just sit out here and do nothing. That's all anyone's ever done on this blasted ship – *nothing*!"

"On the *Axiom,* you will survive," Auto answered mechanically.

The Captain's voice became stronger. "I don't want to survive! I want to *live*!"

Auto replied: "Must follow my directive."

The Captain turned away in frustration. Auto had slowly been taking over the Captain's rightful duties as leader of the *Axiom,* and it was for all the wrong reasons. The Captain turned back and stared at Auto. Then he looked down at the little plant in his lap.

"I'm the Captain of the *Axiom,*" he stated, filled with determination. "We are going home today!"

Auto gave off a series of electronic beeps, and Gopher instantly emerged onto the bridge. Gopher turned towards the Captain. A blue suspension beam suddenly lifted the plant from the Captain's hands.

"Hey, that's my plant!" the Captain yelled at Gopher. "This is mutiny!"

"Probe One," the Captain said to EVE, "arrest Auto!"

And then everything happened very fast. Gopher tossed the plant straight into the trash chute. The Captain gasped. This could not be happening! The plant was gone . . .

. . . until WALL·E appeared. Still climbing up the trash chute, he had caught the plant. He emerged from the chute, looking right at EVE, knowing she would be delighted.

Zzzzap! Auto electrocuted WALL·E. Just like that, the little bot fell to the floor, his circuitry fried. EVE – caught in one of Gopher's suspension beams – watched in horror as WALL·E was dumped down the trash chute.

Still in shock, EVE was barely aware as Gopher disabled her. The Captain gasped as Gopher's beam lifted EVE and unceremoniously threw her down the trash chute!

Turning to the Captain, Auto stated flatly, "You, sir, are confined to quarters."

The out-of-shape Captain was no match for Auto. Despite his attempts to resist, the Captain was pushed down into his quarters. The lights went out. He was now imprisoned without power or access to the outside.

Far below the Captain's quarters, WALL·E and then EVE crashed into the *Axiom*'s waste bay. Tons of trash filled the room. The only light came from the faint orange glow of industrial lamps. Two giant compactor robots made a rumbling sound as they worked. WALL·A was emblazoned on their enormous square chests. They were Waste Allocation Load Lifters, *Axiom* class.

The giants each grabbed a ton of trash, cubed

it, and rotated. They stacked their massive trash cubes on a platform, and the cubes slid on rails into an air lock. The huge air-lock doors started to close with a hiss. Then the exterior hatch flew open, the vacuum of space instantly pulling out the cubed trash.

When EVE awoke, she realized that she and WALL•E were squashed tightly inside two of the giant trash cubes.

Quickly becoming alert, EVE understood the danger that she and WALL•E were in. If they did not get out soon, they would be lost forever in space. She struggled to break free from her trash cube, but she was too tightly wedged inside it. And then – *KA-BLAM!* – EVE used her blaster arm to blow up her trash cube and free herself. But WALL•E was still stuck in his cube.

To make matters worse, all the gigantic trash cubes were now inside the garbage bay's air lock. The outward pull was growing stronger and stronger. They were being sucked out into space!

Finally, EVE managed to pull WALL•E free. But the doors to the air lock were almost closed! M-O, the little cleaner-bot, was still obsessively following his directive, cleaning WALL•E's tracks all the way to the garbage bay. And as the doors were closing, M-O wedged himself between them, keeping them slightly ajar.

The giant WALL•As realized what was happening and moved over to open the doors. M-O was able to get back into the safety of the garbage bay. And EVE, pulling the injured WALL•E, barely made it out of the air lock and through the doors herself. The WALL•As and M-O had helped save WALL•E and EVE.

But WALL•E was badly hurt.

CHAPTER 24

Gently, EVE rested WALL•E against a pile of trash. Opening his chest, she saw that his circuitry had been burnt by Auto's electric blast. She knew she had to do something fast, so she began searching in the junk for a circuit board to replace WALL•E's ruined one.

M-O approached WALL•E. He gently began cleaning him, now as an act of friendship. All this time, M-O had been madly chasing WALL•E, intent on scrubbing him clean. Now he massaged WALL•E's metallic exterior with his softest brush. WALL•E had made M-O see the world differently, too.

EVE returned with a large selection of circuit boards. Then she reached out to hold WALL•E's hand – the one thing he had wanted from her all this time. But instead of giving his hand to her in return, WALL•E offered EVE the plant, which he had kept in his chest cavity.

Struggling to communicate, WALL•E insisted that EVE complete her directive. But EVE no longer cared about her job. She only cared about WALL•E. Tossing the plant aside, she began trying to repair him.

"Rrr." WALL•E struggled to say "Earth." EVE finally understood: If she wanted to repair him, she would have to get him back to Earth, to his home, where he kept all his spare parts.

EVE grabbed the plant. She no longer needed it to complete her directive. She needed it to make the *Axiom* return to Earth so that she could save WALL•E.

Quickly, she scooped up WALL•E and raised her blaster arm to the ceiling. There was a faster way out of this place, but it meant blowing a hole in one of the lower levels of the ship. *BOOM!*

M-O jumped on, too, as EVE flew WALL•E out of the trash bay.

Down in the robot service tunnel, the ship's stewards were feverishly trying to round up the escaped reject-bots, when the entire service hall began to shake. One steward was trying to stop the defective paint-bot from applying yellow lines to the floor. The paint-bot was confusing all the service-bots, who were trying to stay on their lines to follow their directives.

A low rumbling seemed to be coming from far below them. The steward was moving towards the noise when WALL•E, EVE, and M-O burst into the long corridor.

The steward sounded his alarm. He snapped a photo, focusing in on EVE and WALL•E . . . and the plant.

EVE, WALL•E, and M-O took off down the corridor with the paint-bot leaking paint behind them. The paint-bot was humming the song he remembered WALL•E playing in the repair ward.

That gave WALL·E an idea. Still weak and barely functioning, he managed to press the Play button on his chest. The tune echoed faintly through the hallway. But it was enough to lure the timid reject-bots out of hiding. Their hero had returned!

In only moments, the steward's photo had become a WANTED! poster. Images of EVE with WALL·E holding the plant flashed all over the ship. On the bridge, Auto saw the picture. He couldn't believe his eye. "Not possible," he moaned.

Below the bridge, locked in his quarters, the Captain noticed a flash on his computer screen. It was the EVE Probe, the dirty trash-compacting robot . . . and the plant!

The Captain's eyes lit up. A look of determination came over his face. He searched through the manual again and saw a picture of the holo-detector's activation button. Now he knew what he could do to help. He realized that he did not have to put the plant in the holo-detector to set the course for home. The EVE probe could do it without him.

He stared at the ceiling. Somehow, he had to get through that trapdoor and up to the bridge so that he could push the button.

The Captain rolled out of his hover chair, moved under his personal console, and started rewiring his computer. Soon his image and voice showed up on every holo-screen throughout the ship. He was sending a message to EVE.

"Pssst! Hey! Hey! This is the Captain. I'm locked in my room. Probe One, bring the plant to the lido deck. I'll have activated the holo-detector. Now, hurry! Auto's probably going to cut me off, and – "

The air was suddenly filled with static. But EVE and WALL•E had got the message. Instead of heading towards the Captain, they changed direction. They went up towards the lido deck . . . and the holo-detector.

CHAPTER 25

EVE gently held WALL•E and dashed onto the next level, arriving at the courtyard of the economy-class deck. A wall of stewards came forward and tried to block their path. "Halt!" a steward shouted. Behind him, other stewards stood ready to use their freeze rays to stop WALL•E and EVE in their tracks.

The mob of reject-bots sprang into action. They would do anything for WALL•E. The defective beautician-bot lunged forward. Using her hand mirrors, she deflected the oncoming barrage of freeze rays. Umbrella-bots took up the cause and snapped open, protecting WALL•E, EVE, and the throng of reject-bots behind them.

On the bridge, Auto watched as the stewards'

blips disappeared from his screen. Certain that things couldn't get any worse, Auto was astounded to see the image of the Captain appear on his screen. And the Captain was holding the plant!

"Ha! Ha! Look what I got, Auto!" the Captain said, taunting him. "That's right! The plant!"

"Not possible," Auto answered angrily, his eye going wide.

The Captain was tricking Auto. He didn't have the real plant. He was merely projecting the image of the plant taken from EVE's memory chip into his hands.

"You want it?" the Captain said, hoping Auto would take the bait. "Come and get it, Blinky!"

The portal in the Captain's ceiling suddenly snapped open and Auto shot down into the room. Auto's eye saw nothing.

"Captain?" Auto said, cautiously searching the dark room. Suddenly, the Captain leaped at Auto. He grabbed on to the machine and refused to let go as Auto dragged him around the room.

"Let go! Let go!" Auto yelled. Auto thrashed wildly and finally yanked the Captain up through the portal in the ceiling and onto the bridge.

"You're not getting away from me, One-Eye!" the Captain shouted. He reached for the big blue button as he and Auto flailed around the bridge.

"That's it! A little closer," the Captain grunted. "Must . . . push . . . button!"

All of a sudden, Gopher popped out of his pneumatic tube and saw the fight. He immediately charged towards the Captain.

Auto whipped the Captain around, accidentally hitting Gopher with the Captain's foot. The force sent Gopher crashing through the control-room window. With his siren screaming, Gopher landed in a heap on the lido deck below.

CHAPTER 26

EVE flew WALL·E through the economy-class level of the *Axiom*. The humming throng of reject-bots was happily following them. They still needed to get up to the lido deck, which was past the main concourse and the coach-class deck.

Then another crowd of stewards appeared. They launched a web of freeze rays, locking down WALL·E, EVE, and the reject-bots.

But the Captain was not giving up. Working harder than he had in his entire life, he struggled against Auto up on the bridge. Finally, still clinging to Auto, the Captain managed to get one hand free . . . and smacked the blue button.

"Ha! Ha! Gotcha!" the Captain yelled to Auto.

As the alarm sounded all over the ship, the *Axiom*'s automated systems prepared the passengers for their return flight to Earth. Hover chairs carrying passengers poured out of the guest suites.

The stewards toppled, crushed by the uncontrollable onslaught of hover chairs heading up to the lido deck. And when the stewards fell, their freeze rays dissolved, freeing WALL•E, EVE, and the reject-bots.

EVE quickly resumed course, cradling the weakened WALL•E. The reject-bots followed close behind. At last, they reached the lido deck.

A huge cylinder rose from the floor. It was the holo-detector.

The entire ship's population was gathering. Passengers lined the balconies on all sides, and the floor was filled to capacity.

The giant video screen in the fake sky flashed on. Everyone looked up and saw the Captain.

"Ladies . . . and gentlemen!" the Captain said,

gasping as Auto knocked him into the console. "Remain seated. Just a slight delay. Stand by!"

The passengers were confused. Mary looked around and saw several toddlers in their hover rings. All the commotion had frightened them. She and John rushed over. They soothed the toddlers, then passed them to other passengers in hover chairs.

Above them, the huge video screen continued to broadcast the struggle between the Captain and Auto. Auto seemed to be getting the upper hand. The entire ship tilted to one side. Passengers tumbled from their chairs, but WALL·E managed to hold on to the holo-detector.

Pushed to the side of the ship, EVE saw a monorail car fall off its track. She looked around. Mary and many of the children were next to her. They were in the sliding monorail's path.

EVE needed to place the plant in the holo-detector. But she wanted to help the passengers, too.

EVE zoomed towards the monorail and, using both hands, held it back. The plant, now slipping away, was lost somewhere on the tilting deck. To make matters worse, sliding passengers piled up against the monorail, adding more weight as EVE struggled to hold the car up.

Up on the bridge, Auto kept the ship tilted.

Then he switched the holo-detector button off.

The leaning holo-detector began moving back down into the deck. WALL•E barely held on. He wedged himself under one side of the holo-detector, trying to keep it from closing up. The pressure squished WALL•E into a box. Damaged as he already was, WALL•E refused to give up.

From the bridge, Auto could see that the holo-detector was jammed. He saw WALL•E struggling against the hydraulics of the huge cylinder.

"No!" Auto cried.

The Captain watched helplessly as Auto repeatedly pushed the holo-detector button. Looking up at Auto's screen, the Captain saw

WALL•E being crushed. The passengers were screaming as the tilting ship tossed them around.

The Captain grasped the console's rails and pulled himself up to his wobbly feet. Standing, he looked around the control room. He'd never seen things from this position before.

Breathlessly, the passengers watched the giant screen. The Captain was actually standing! He took a step and then began to walk. The crowd cheered wildly.

Auto turned to see what the fuss was about and found himself face to face with the Captain. They had never been at eye level before. Auto stared, stunned, as the Captain lifted a finger . . . and turned off Auto's power. It was just that simple.

"Noooo," Auto moaned as his eye faded out for good. The Captain smiled triumphantly. The passengers roared, beaming with pride at their new hero.

CHAPTER 27

The Captain took command of the bridge. He grabbed the ship's wheel and turned it. Passengers spilled across the lido deck as the *Axiom* levelled itself.

EVE set the monorail down and zoomed over to WALL•E. He was pinned under the edge of the holo-detector. She tried to lift it, but it wouldn't budge. It was still closing, crushing WALL•E in the process.

EVE looked for the plant. She knew that if the holo-detector closed, she would never be able to save WALL•E. Suddenly, from across the deck, she heard a robot calling out to her. It was M-O! He raised the plant for her to see from across the lido deck. EVE waved as M-O teamed up with the reject-bots, who worked with the humans to pass the plant to EVE. Every one of them had been inspired in some way by WALL·E.

EVE grasped the plant and fitted it – at the last possible second – into the sinking holo-detector.

The detector scanned the plant. "Plant origin identified," the ship's computer said. "Global reparation complete. Set course for Earth."

The lido deck's sky suddenly became transparent, revealing the sea of stars floating in space. The passengers gasped, and one by one, they began to take in the world beyond their own tight confines. The red coordinates for Earth glowed against the darkness of outer space as the ship's computer announced, "Hyperjump in twenty seconds."

The holo-detector rose. EVE's directive had been completed. The *Axiom* would return to Earth!

But the happy moment was lost when WALL·E toppled out from underneath the holo-detector.

He was in even worse shape than before – badly crushed and leaking oil. EVE looked at him and gasped.

"WALL•E?" EVE said, trying to take his hand. But WALL•E was fading. His hand dropped from hers.

EVE hardly noticed as the ship's computer began the countdown: "Ten . . . nine . . . eight . . ."

She just tried to hold on to WALL•E as the *Axiom* jumped to its fastest speed. She had seen him repair himself with the spare parts in his home on Earth. She would take him there. And she would try to bring him back to life.

Up on the bridge, the stars streaked by and the delighted Captain steered the ship and held on for the high-speed ride to Earth.

CHAPTER 28

On the broken flyover where his master had left him, WALL·E's lonely cockroach was still obediently waiting.

Suddenly, a red dot appeared on the ground. Gently at first, the ground began to shake. The little roach looked back at the sky. A dark shape was growing, blotting out the Sun. Slowly, the giant keel of the *Axiom* broke through the clouds, throwing the entire landscape into shadow.

Hundreds of glowing red dots rushed past. The excited cockroach could sense that his master was close to home and eagerly chased after the dots. Above him, the sleek city-sized star liner gracefully descended from the sky.

The earth shuddered. Towers of trash tumbled

as the *Axiom* set down, home at last.

A row of giant doors on the side of the ship slid open. Multiple gangways extended from each doorway to the ground.

The Captain was the first to take a tentative step outside the ship. The other passengers stood at the tops of the gangways, unwilling to leave the ship. They looked out at Earth's skyline for the first time.

"I don't know about this," one passenger said.

"Can't we stay on the ship?" said another.

The crowd grew nervous, hurling questions at the Captain and one another. "We came eight million miles for this?" "Can they turn the lights down?" "It's getting kind of warm."

"At least it's a dry heat," one passenger noted.

Then EVE appeared. She flew outside, clutching WALL·E tightly in her arms. The reject-bots followed behind her. The battered, boxed-up little WALL·E unit was almost home.

EVE paused at the bottom of the gangway. WALL•E's happy little cockroach saw his master . . . and realized that something was wrong. He rushed up and jumped onto EVE's back, inching close to WALL•E.

EVE looked out over the landscape. Scanning the vast dry bay, she spotted WALL•E's deserted truck. The sooner she could get to WALL•E's spare parts, the sooner she could fix him. She took to the sky and zoomed across the bay, with the reject-bots following below in the sludge, trying unsuccessfully to keep up.

WALL•E's treasures jingled on the shelves as the back door slowly opened. EVE flew in and set WALL•E on his back. She quickly scoured the rotating shelves and found WALL•E's collection of spare parts.

Using a rusty car jack, she ratcheted up WALL•E's crushed body and grabbed the spare parts. With sparks flying, EVE frantically began to repair WALL•E.

Finally, she placed new solar panels on WALL•E, raised her blaster arm, and blew a hole in the truck's roof. A shaft of sunlight beamed down on WALL•E as EVE held her breath and watched. Would the solar rays give him the energy he needed?

The reject-bots, still trying to catch up with EVE, saw the explosion that erupted from WALL•E's truck. Back at the ship, the Captain also saw it. But he kept moving forward, carrying the plant. When he reached a spot of soil at the bottom of a gangway, he knelt down and began digging a hole. When he felt that it was deep enough, he gently placed his precious plant inside, carefully patting the soil in around the stem. It was one tiny plant, but it was a beginning.

Meanwhile, the reject-bots kept racing towards WALL•E's truck.

And inside the truck, EVE waited. At first, nothing happened. Then she heard one faint beep; then another. WALL•E's head slowly rose out of his box, and his big eyes blinked open. The cockroach jumped up and down. His robot master was alive!

EVE looked at WALL•E and held out her hand to him.

"WALL•E," she hummed softly.

But WALL•E didn't answer. He stared at her blankly. EVE pointed to herself, saying, "EVE, EVE." WALL•E looked at her for a moment, then rotated his head away.

This couldn't be happening! EVE tried to show WALL•E some of his favourite collections, but he didn't seem to care. He simply wanted to gather them like trash and compact them into cubes. He had become just another WALL•E unit, following his directive.

"No!" EVE cried, frustrated and angry, as she watched him roll outside. After all this time, all that WALL•E had done . . . how could he be gone, just a shell of his former self? It wasn't fair.

Sadly, EVE followed him outside and leaned

her head against his. She closed her eyes and grieved because love, the real spark of life, had left his robot heart.

As EVE held WALL•E's hand – the only thing he had ever really wanted from her – a spark of energy passed between their heads – a robot kiss.

EVE felt WALL•E wiggle his hand. Looking into his eyes, she saw some light returning to them. He began to focus. His hand clasped hers more tightly.

She saw the real WALL•E's eyes blink to life.

"Eee-vah?" he said as his eyes widened.

"WALL•E!" she cried. The reject-bots had finally arrived, and now they cheered. The cockroach chirped happily.

And as WALL•E's favourite song played from inside his truck, another tiny arc of electricity sparked between him and EVE. WALL•E's moment had finally arrived. As he held EVE's hand, he felt her squeeze his in return.

CHAPTER 29

As the Sun set behind the *Axiom,* the Captain led the rest of his passengers down the ramp.

"C'mon, everyone," he said heartily. "It's one small step for man, one giant – " But before he could take the next step, his small feet went out from under him and he tumbled down the ramp.

A steward-bot chased after him, shouting, "Please remain stationary!"

The passengers watched as the stewards surrounded their captain. Straining, he raised himself to his feet.

"No, no, I'm all right, I can do it myself." The Captain didn't want any help. And as he stood and dusted himself off, the crowd was filled with a kind of pride that had long been forgotten.

"Okay," he said to his passengers, who were now eager to follow his lead. "We're going to dig the water well here." He pointed to the empty bay and took in the desolate horizon. "And dig the food well over there.

"Ahhh," he said, smiling, knowing that humans and their planet had been given another chance. "This is going to be great!"

The Captain was right. He and his passengers would soon find out that another change had taken place. Off on a distant mountain of trash, a green field of tiny plants was sprouting.

Across the bay, WALL·E and EVE sat on the roof of his truck, happily watching the Sun set over planet Earth. WALL·E would never really understand how he had caused so much change just by following his heart. But holding hands with EVE, surrounded by a throng of joyful reject-bots, he knew that, finally, everything in the universe was as it should be.